MYSTERY MINUTES

VOLUME 1

B. A. PAUL

Contents

FOREWORD

Ready for some mind-boggling math?

There are two sides to every story.

If the above statement is true, logic dictates there's my version of events and yours. If we were the only two "there." For sake of illustration, let's say "there" means at the library when the book stacks caught fire.

And let's say *you* sat the stacks on fire. (Sorry, someone's gotta be the "bad" guy, and I don't think I'd have the guts to burn books in the library during business hours). You though, I wouldn't put it past you...

So now, there's my eye-witness account (which is clouded by my high emotional state and my perception of you, not to mention smoke inhalation), there's your story (clouded by your emotional state, your perception of the events, and smoke inhalation), there's Mr. Librarian's side along with two other patrons' versions, equally clouded by their elevated emotional states, their perceptions of you and me and the library, and, no doubt, smoke inhalation.

Now how many sides are there?

Five people in a setting that's on fire.

Five sides to the story?

Or are there ten? The version that each actually experienced with their senses—no filters or emotions attached (you came in, you burned the stacks) and the OMG! I just about died version (the one where they swear you were ranting and raving and giving dirty looks, and, and, and...)

Even if one were trying to be objective, there's the trouble with the five senses. Not all five are firing at optimum capacity for each witness at any given moment, so maybe those sides of the story aren't worth much. Someone forgot their glasses or turned down their hearing aid. One patron came to the library to sleep off an all-night bender so his wife wouldn't yell, so none of his senses are reliable.

Let's just take me. My version is skewed because I'm ticked at you for burning the stacks. I'm also scared out of my mind because you nearly set us both aflame, and I can't think straight because I'm having trouble breathing. But maybe you're my best friend so I'll fabricate an additional storyline to tell the fire department because I don't want you to get in trouble. Even though I thought it was over the top that you would use arson to make a point to Mr. Librarian who dumped you, my best friend, on *Valentine's Day* even, to go out with the technician from the CDC (who's in town to investigate a biological hazard in the school across the street from the library). I get why you're ticked. I mean, those two just met...

In only *my* head, there's what I think I saw (which may differ from what you actually did), what I'll tell everyone else I saw (a version of the story, but perhaps not a totally accurate one,) and last but not least, the version I'll tell myself so I can sleep better at night (perhaps the oversized water bottle in my backpack would have doused the situation before it got out of control. I just won't mention that I had the means to stop it lest I'm implicated too...).

That's three stories in one head. How many do you have? Three? Two? One? What about the librarian? His version of what happened must be skewed because now he's afraid you'll show up (or send me since you're likely going to jail) to burn his house to the ground while he sleeps...

Maybe he's so afraid of you, that he'll tell the fire chief that *I'm* the one that set the stacks on fire. And since I was standing so close to you when you did it, I'm covered in evidence, so the story would fit.

Or maybe the angle was off from the point of view of one of the patrons. And they saw Mr. Librarian in the stacks last. And that patron overheard Mr. Librarian talking with his boss about how upset he was that he didn't get off work early on Valentine's Day to take Little Miss CDC to a nicer place to eat.

How many sides are there to every story? As many as the human mind, emotional state, and motive can muster. This makes for great fiction. Thrillers and mysteries and dramas would run cold if there were only one side.

For real life (and I've had fantastically more than my share of real life lately), I wish there were a formula. Plug each eye witness's tainted memories, emotional baggage, and skewed motives into one side of the equation, and out pops absolute truth on the other. Then everyone knows "the rest of the story." But alas, we're left to wonder and ponder and lose sleep over drama and dilemmas with no answers.

Meanwhile, what no one knows is that you did it because Little Miss CDC was a terrorist who'd unleashed a biohazard virus into those stacks and you sat the library on fire to kill the deadly bug and save thousands of lives at the expense of a few books. But your fire destroyed the evidence of that bug, and you're now sitting in jail because everyone else's versions fit better.

And Little Miss CDC gets away.

But you're very happy that I didn't douse your flame with my water bottle before the fire overtook the stacks. Because thousands would've died a horrible death.

And because I didn't use that water bottle, I'm now the hero of my own twisted tale.

At least that's how I'll tell it if anyone should ask.

Happy reading!

B. A. Paul

Detective Zane and the Case of the Pink Hats

Detective Zane thought working the streets of Denver was a challenge. But not even that beat could prepare him for the Florida heat and the moody creatures of Happy Tails Animal Rescue.

"Hey, Zane, we need help over at Lola's." Zane's walkie rattled its staticky request where it hung from his leather belt. It had taken him a while to get used to the weight of the thing. It was off by several ounces from the piece that hung there three years ago—or was it four years now? Four years of working these grounds. And he'd taken to wearing the walkie around the house, feeling naked without it when doing dishes or laundry.

The more likely scenario: He just missed his gun.

He shoved the memory away and pushed the talk button. "Okay, Dwight. Be there in a few."

"Now would be better. We've had an incident *inside*."

Inside.

Zane wondered what Lola did this time. He locked the metal door to the small office the employees jokingly called "Command Central" as he stepped from the poorly air-conditioned building into the Florida humidity. After years of humanity's accomplishments— men on the moon, probes to Mars, and Twinkies—you'd think that someone could figure out humidity. Eradicate this particular element from the equation.

There'd be less crime. Heat does crazy things to people. He nodded to Cliff as the old man emptied the trash bins along the pathways. The old guy reminded Zane of everyone's grandfather. A tease and a cut-up, tall and lanky. Paling blue eyes of old age.

And bored out of his gourd, hence the part-time work. "Need more help, boss," Cliff called and shook his head as he wrestled a liner into a can. "Lots of bins. Lots of messes."

"Workin' on it."

Cliff, the newest—and only—addition the management would add to staff this year for budget reasons. Zane had given lists of safety concerns to them since he'd started this post. But no one listened. Not even about the glitchy security cameras.

He hopped into the open-aired jeep and floored it—as quickly as one could floor it amongst the guests, food carts, and junk toy vendors—over to Lola's.

Lola. He'd only had to tangle with her once before on her side of the gate. He tried to keep his distance. Mean as a tiger and quite fast for her age, she was as unpredictable and as grumpy as any menopausal woman in his family—and his family was full of menopausal women.

A crowd of mothers and children had gathered in front of Lola's enclosure. He honked the horn three times fast to spread the bodies, threw the Jeep into park, and dropped onto the pavement. A hysterical woman paced from one edge of the gate to the other, a small screaming boy balanced on her hip. "Where is she, where is she? That's her hat, but I don't see her!"

Dwight was already securing Lola's snout with a tattered leather strap, his knees resting near each of her temples, and his trainee, Michelle, straddled the old gal's midsection, her bare legs covered in mud up to the hem of her shorts. Gatorade, Lola's man, was twenty feet away nearer the shelter than the fence and frantic crowd. The pair had been fed a juicy hindquarter of deer before opening time and must've been docile enough for the two-person crew to wrangle without much incident.

"Emily!" The mother was screaming over and over. The child in her arms echoed her volume, as did a couple of toddlers in the crowd.

Zane assessed the situation quickly. Gatorade could care less about what was happening, and Lola was secured. So his crew inside the exhibit was safe.

He looked over the wire mesh fencing at the shallow canal that snaked through the enclosure. At the murky water's edge was a bright pink sun hat, half in the mud and half in the water. No body—or parts of a body—could be seen on the land portions of the enclosure. Just two employees, two gators, and one hat.

Michelle dismounted Lola and retrieved the hat. Next to Michelle's feet, dark brown stains where breakfast had been served an hour ago.

"Ma'am." Zane took the woman's shoulders and turned her away from the enclosure to face him as Michelle and Dwight approached the canal. Tears drug mascara from her eyes all the way to her jawline. The boy's face was a mess of snot and tears. "I need you to stop screaming and tell me what you saw."

"Emily was here. Just right here." She wiggled away from Zane's loose hold and started to act out where she and her children were when Emily went missing. "She was at my hip, then she was gone, and her hat was over there." She pulled back to the fence and yelled her daughter's name again. Zane repeated his attempt at getting her to focus.

"But did you actually *see* her go over the fence?" He had a hard time believing that in a crowd this size a little one would have the chance to scale the barrier without someone intervening. Especially with all the undoubtedly protective mothers in attendance today.

"I don't know. I don't know." She sobbed.

"What was she wearing?" Zane motioned for an overly curious onlooker to gather the frantic mother and boy and move them to the bench opposite the gator display. The mother managed to spit out Emily's wardrobe: white top, pink shorts. Blonde curly hair.

"Please sit here while we look. I promise I'll keep you updated." He gave his new "assistant" a please-don't-let-her-over-there look, and the older woman seemed to understand his silent plea, and he used his walkie to communicate with the rest of the park's employees to be on the lookout.

But the hat was over the fence. He wasn't sure the rest of the park needed to know the girl's description.

Zane walked back to the Jeep and phoned the local police for help in crowd control. He also retrieved the megaphone to attempt to push back the onlookers with the standard "please give us room to work and be respectful of the mother" instructions.

"Hey, she didn't like that!" Dwight yelled from the enclosure. The megaphone's blast and squeal had sent Lola's tail into a hostile warning wave and she turned toward the canal where Michelle stood examining the water. Zane ditched the mega to the back seat of the Jeep and retrieved his enclosure keys.

He'd sweat through his shirt on the sixty-second drive from Command. He'd sweat through it again talking to the mother, and now that he was about to enter the gate, he thought the sweat would soak through the tips of his steel-toed boots. He opened the gate and locked it closed behind him, cursing the Powers that Be under his breath for not listening to his requests for Happy Tails—their little animal-rehab-gone-mini-zoo establishment. He'd thought about calling Cliff over to help while they waited on the police, but the custodian moved about as fast as the giant land tortoise two exhibits down, and the entire incident would be resolved before Cliff could figure out which direction to go.

Zane tucked the bottoms of his khakis inside his boots. Four feet of mud-caked grass lining the fence gave way to the canal, which Zane waded into without outward hesitation, training from a previous life rewiring him for the task at hand. Inward hesitation he had plenty of, and no amount of past—or current—training could erase that.

He feared what his shins may meet under the three feet of murky water. Two gators made this place home. An unknown number of snakes claimed the same real estate.

More than that, he feared stubbing up against the mangled or—dead—body of a little girl.

Michelle stood a few feet from him on the opposite bank, dripping pink sun hat in her shaking hand. The blood around her boots had mostly soaked into the ground. She saw his face and said, "This is the spot where we fed them this morning. That's not necessarily..."

Zane could tell she had her doubts. Zane could also tell Gatorade was now more interested in the commotion than he had been a few minutes ago. His toothy snout aimed in their direction while Lola swung her massive tail back and forth like a scaly cat preparing to pounce on a fledgling.

He held up his hand to Michelle and waved her up the side of the bank. "Keep an eye on those two. I'll walk the water." She nodded and turned to help Dwight wrangle gators if the need should arise. Dwight had retrieved a second leather strap to secure Gatorade's mouth. He and Michelle stood with their backs to the water, watching the lizards, and gave Zane the all-clear.

Zane kept one hand on his hip, the other rested on top of his walkie. How he wished it was his service revolver. Or anything other than a walkie. He began taking sweeping sideways steps through the canal. He glanced back toward the fence a few times, making sure Emily's mother wasn't in sight. The crowd had not listened—as is customary for crowds—and was beginning to fill the spaces along the fence with worried and curious faces. He focused on what he was doing and prayed the boys in blue would hurry it up.

A couple of times his boot brushed against something, and he'd carefully used his toe to bring the objects to the surface. So far, a broken tree branch and an algae-covered deer or bovine femur—he thought.

He walked the short canal several times over the next ten minutes. In that time, two police officers had arrived and started barking orders at the crowd, which still didn't want to cooperate.

"I don't see anything. Not one thing," Zane said to the others.

"I'm not seeing any signs of fresh food. No ripped clothing. No hair." Dwight had examined both gators' strapped mouths while Zane drug the canal.

One of the boys up top had evidently given up on unassisted verbal commands and had commandeered Zane's megaphone. "Ladies and gentlemen, if you could please step away from the—"

The shrill tone of the mega sent Lola's tail and feet into high gear. She lunged toward the water—toward Zane. His heart, already struggling to keep its proper position in Zane's chest, flip-flopped to her padding rhythm and he could feel the beats all the way to his wet feet. Michelle wasn't enough to thwart her, and Lola, followed closely now by an agitated Gatorade, made for the water a little faster, knocking Michelle to her butt near the water's edge with one fast swoop of her tail.

Zane kept his eyes on the gators while he backed up to the opposite bank against the fencing. "Stop using that thing. Turn it off," Zane barked as he scrambled to keep his footing on the slick mud. Dwight jumped on Gatorade's back and Michelle found her feet in time to help him secure the male.

But Lola was locked on like a laser to a target, swishing her tail and head, trying to rid herself of her bond and rid the enclosure of the intruder.

One officer scaled the fence and landed at Zane's side. "What do we do now?"

Zane didn't know. His mind raced, one thought bumping into the next. He was security, not animal handler. He was a Coloradoan, not a Floridian. He knew how to hunt for bodies, not ward off dragons. And he had a walkie, not a gun. "Don't get eaten," was all he could offer.

He and the policeman side-stepped along the fence toward the gate as Zane fished for his keys and the officer yelled at the crowd to make way—and they listened this time, backing up to give the men room to exit the gator display.

Or more likely, to make space for Lola's exit from the enclosure if she made it across the canal.

Lola was closing in, her body halfway in the water, still trying to fight the leather strap around her snout. Zane thought he could see more daylight between the leather and her hide as she worked to loosen its hold and he worked to loosen the correct key.

He found the one and slid it into the lock as her body slid all the way into the murk. He looked over his shoulder as the officer crowded and hurried him. Nothing more disturbing than losing sight of one's enemy. He'd liked it better when he could see her pearly whites hanging out of her jowls than when he couldn't see any of her.

The gate finally gave, and the men stumbled onto pavement and slammed it shut. Lola slowly floated to the top of the canal, her eyes bugging out of her reptilian head. She'd lost her strap in the water. Zane shouted for the other two to get out of the enclosure, to which they had no objections. Gatorade was secured, and Lola started up the opposite side of the water after them as they reached the enclosure's access building at the back. Once his people were safe, he faced the crowd, who stared in a unified gawk.

As he rounded the back of the press toward the bench, the mother, boy, and older woman were still seated. No longer hysterical.

Next to them, Cliff stood smiling with his arm around a little girl with blonde curls wearing pink shorts and a white top. Licking a vanilla ice cream cone.

And a spotless, bright pink sun hat.

The police officers had cleared away the congestion, sending visitors to other areas of the park. The reunited family was shaken, but no harm done at all. Cliff had found the girl crying by one of the unmanned vendor carts. She'd likely seen the bright images of ice cream on the front and had wandered from mom and brother to check it out. No one had seen her leave the alligator showcase. And everyone had assumed she'd gone over.

No eyewitnesses. No one ever sees anything when they live behind the screens of their cell phones.

Zane signed some paperwork for the cops and thanked them for their assistance. Cliff had returned to his never-ending duties after some of the younger employees showered him with hugs and hi-fives for finding the girl. He loved the attention, and Zane imagined it was hard for Cliff to go back to the work. Some of the girls from the gate even called him "Pops." Everyone's grandfather.

The family had retreated to their car, the boy complaining that he'd not seen the "lelepants," but mom had had enough.

Zane had had enough, as well. And there was still the question of the pink hat found in the gator exhibit.

"It wasn't there yesterday. It wasn't there this morning. We'd have seen it when we fed them." Dwight waved a newspaper in front of his face in a feeble attempt to circulate more cool air. He and Michelle had joined Zane in the drier climate of Happy Tails Command Central to decompress and evaluate. They all downed water from sweaty plastic bottles, then refilled again from the tap in mini kitchen tucked in the corner of the office.

Dwight seemed certain, and Zane believed him. Michelle was there, shadowing him the whole time as well, and between the two of them, the most competent workers in the park, he had no doubt that the hat went over sometime early this morning after the visitors entered the main gates.

"Does that mean we're still missing a child?" Michelle was still shaken. She'd taken on the unpaid trainee position to pad her resume, hopeful for employment at one of the Disney parks in return for her efforts this summer. Zane wondered if she was rethinking her career choice.

He knew he was. This was supposed to be a less stressful—albeit hotter—gig than policing the back alleyways of Denver. Especially after that last missing person's case. A little girl. A little girl that someone should have seen wander off. And then another girl can't be found. And then Zane found the bodies and had stopped sleeping. And then he'd stopped eating.

And then, and then. And then this.

An opportunity to erase the visual reminders of his past nightmares. Right down to the climate.

But it was happening again. Looking for a little girl mangled by wildlife instead of wild men.

Michelle handed Zane the hat that she'd not let out of her sight since picking it out of the canal.

"I don't think so." It had been over an hour since Emily's disappearance and no one had reported a missing child. There was no evidence of anything amiss in Lola's exhibit. *Someone would have seen...*

"Someone probably thought it would be funny to toss it over to get Lola or Gatorade's attention," Dwight said. He had an entire Rubbermaid tote full of choking hazards in the gator storage shed. Some cell phones and cameras dropped innocently enough. Other things—soda cans, cigarette packs, ink pens—thrown over the fence out of pure disrespect for the animals and disregard for the safety of the staff that had to clean it up. "But it's a good thing you did that sweep through the canal, boss. That'll keep the Righties off our tails for a bit, anyway."

Michelle stood from her seat and paced. Zane knew the feeling. Lots of anxious energy had to go somewhere—and she was the least experienced one of the three. She gave Zane and Dwight a nervous smile and refilled her water bottle before sitting down again.

"Maybe it will," Zane said to Dwight's remark. The Righties, as Dwight called them, were the multiple animal rights activist groups that flooded the Happy Tails and other parks like it, protesting and generally causing disruption of business. No matter how many tours the Righties' leaders were given behind the scenes, no matter how many documents were produced, Zane and the owners couldn't seem to keep them at bay. Happy Tails was a rehab-first facility. They didn't take in animals from the wild on whims to make a profit. If they had made a profit, they'd have more staff and security cameras that didn't zone out during business hours.

No, no profit here. Happy Tails took in animals that weren't fit for release into the wild because some idiot thought it'd be a good idea to raise a bear as a house pet. Or urban development near the swampland displaced discombobulated scaly mammoths who helped themselves to Shit-Tzu snacks from backyards and refused to be rezoned, resulting in two bullets to the back side—Lola. Or those who terrorized golf courses and required surgery to remove *eighteen* golf balls from his gut—Gatorade.

Some animals had been housed in poorly kept establishments and were rehomed here for overall better living conditions. Happy Tails had giraffes and elephants and a dozen other assorted misfit adoptees.

But you couldn't convince some of the more misguided activist groups of this. That's why Dwight had named them "Righties." They were always right even in the face of irrefutable proof.

"Maybe," Zane said again and stood to stretch. "I'll drive you two back to the lizards."

"Thanks. We'd better get the strap off of Gatorade before they catch wind of *that*." Dwight said. "You be okay to go back for another round?" He nodded toward Michelle, who was just getting the color back in her cheeks.

"Sure, boss."

"Hear that Zane? She called *me* boss."

"I hear ya. Get in the Jeep."

Outside, the crowds were a little lighter, the approaching afternoon heat and rolling gray clouds to the west driving animals into lethargic existences in whatever shade they could find and keeping housewives home with their brood. He drove Dwight and Michelle back; Lola was floating in her moat. Gatorade was still, the strap tight around his mouth. "Careful."

"You, too."

Zane planned on circling the zoo, making note of any other issues that crept up during the morning and contacting the management yet again. He rounded the corner by Nellie, the tortoise, when his walkie fired off another alarmed plea for help.

"Hey, Zane. We got a problem." It was Mike. "Elmar's upset. Stomping. Throwing dirt. Found a hat. A little girl's hat. The teens that saw the hat are causing a ruckus, but I can't see a kid."

You've gotta be kidding me. "I'll be right there." He pressed the gas a little harder, honking as he went, hoping Gatorade—or Lola— didn't become agitated at the sound of his horn.

As he approached the elephant paddock, a small crowd of a dozen or so—not nearly the size of the one earlier—was hanging as close to the fence as possible, fingers through the wires and noses pressed in close. He decided to leave the megaphone alone and just push them aside. "Is everyone here okay? Anyone missing?" The crowd consisted mainly of teens, some he recognized as season pass holders. None of them troublemakers as far as he knew. They all shook their heads.

"Yeah, but did some kid get in there? Look at that!"

Elmar was stomping and swaying like Zane had never witnessed before. The other two elephants huddled shoulder to shoulder under the large shade tree watching Elmar like he'd gone mad. Mike was dusting off a pink hat.

A bright pink sunhat identical to the one sitting on Zane's desk back at Command.

"Did one of you throw that over?" Zane demanded of the teenagers. They all shook their heads. "Cause if you did, that's a serious issue and could cause you possible jail time."

All headshakes again.

Zane wasn't as sure about his troublemaker assessment as he was when he first approached them. He requested they leave as rumbles of thunder sounded off in the distance. They didn't argue and dispersed down the pathways toward the entrance of Happy Tails.

Zane wasn't sure of his abilities at all at the moment. Four years off the force had filled him with all kinds of doubts.

Doubt about reading people being at the top of the list at the moment.

As Mike approached the fence to squeeze the hat through the wires, Zane's walkie went off again. He took the crumpled hat and answered the call.

Another hat in the giraffe exhibit. Pink.

That was it. He drove the Jeep back to Command and made the judgment call to shut down the park. He sent word out over the walkies to the crew members to assist guests to the front gates and to make sure every guest was accounted for. That no parents were missing any children.

He flipped the switch over the park-wide speaker system and told the guests that Happy Tails was closing early due to severe incoming weather and would issue rainchecks at the front gates.

He watched out the window as the crowds grew thick toward the front of the park. He laid Elmar's pink hat, dusty and trampled, next to Lola's muddy one.

Two hats. One temporarily missing girl. One miserable coincidence.

One more hat to collect from Stretch's exhibit.

One more that he knew of.

And only half of the cameras in the park were operational at any given moment.

God only knew which half.

Zane was wrong. The crew found three more hats in addition to the three he knew about. Six hats, all over the park. All in enclosures. And one very sick wolf who'd snacked on half of a hat in between her regular meals.

He pulled off his sweat- and mud-stained khakis and unbuttoned his uniform shirt. He stood directly on top of the AC vent in the bathroom of his studio apartment and let the cool air dry him off and stop the sweat glands from pouring before he got into the shower.

After he showered he stood naked over the vent again until the chill reached his bones. Like winter in Denver.

He'd phoned the police officer, Warren, who'd helped him earlier in the day just to keep them apprised of the situation. Legal matters would be pending if they caught the moron tossing hats in with the animals. It puts the critters at risk. Just ask Meteor about her belly ache.

And it put the staff in even more danger. His staff. His team. Just ask Michelle. And Zane.

He requested that the night watchman patrol every twenty minutes throughout his shift as opposed to hourly. Brent wasn't too happy about it, since the extra rounds would seriously hinder his online poker progress. But Zane insisted, and Brent had agreed.

Zane dressed in the lightest-weight clothing he could find and poured himself a bowl of cereal. He sat down at the table in front of the six pink hats he'd brought home with him—with Officer Warren's permission, since any evidence had been trampled or chewed away.

He chewed and contemplated. He breathed deeply between bites, trying to let the stress of the day go and to remember his training. Four years at Happy Tails and he'd gotten the typical job stress that comes with any job. Different personalities don't quite get along. A ruckus or two in a crowd. A sick animal now and then. Crappy security tech and low staff numbers.

But this, this is the closest he'd come to having to tap into his pre-Happy Tails life. He'd need to become Detective Zane Frasier again. Denver PD.

Yes, he knew the stakes weren't as high. He wasn't talking about missing person cases—although he thought it had come to that earlier this morning with Emily. The animals, as special and quirky as they are, weren't too high up on his risk-your-life-for-it scale, but the humans were. Humans like Michelle and Dwight and the potential other crew members who'd be injured or worse just doing their jobs.

And he would try his best to keep the Righties off the war path that led to Happy Tails.

He couldn't stomach any more cereal. He slurped a few sips of the leftover fruity milk and sat the bowl down.

He picked up the first hat—Lola's hat—and examined it. Small, child-sized, as were all of them. Part muddy, part murky canal stained. He turned it inside out and found a tiny embroidered maker's mark. He did the same with the rest, except Meteor's. She'd eaten the half with the label. All the hats had come from the same maker: Marla's Marvels.

He jotted down some notes detective-style—except the notes were on the back of a takeout menu—and grabbed his laptop to search for the name on the inside of the hats.

A local place. A little mom-and-pop boutique with "Mom" Marla selling the cloth goods aimed at tourists' children and "Pop" crafting wooden signs with burnt-in etchings of "Wish you Were Here" and "My Friends Went to Florida and All I Got was This Stupid Sign".

Seriously, how do places like this afford the rent in strip malls? Zane shook his head and programmed the address into his cell phone. He'd visit the place in the morning before his shift.

There wasn't much to be done this evening. He stretched and took his bowl to the sink and retrieved his keys from the entryway hook. He recharged the walkie and plugged in his cell. Zane divided his sleeping area from the rest of the studio with a series of square cubbies, some hollow and some solid. The hollow ones were either empty or held a random book or decoration. Mostly junk from Happy Tails gifted to him by thankful field trip teachers.

The solid-backed cubbies faced open toward his bed, where he kept only a few mementoes of his life in Denver.

A souvenir shot glass from when the guys took him to The Cruise Room to celebrate making Detective.

A group photo of him with those same guys on the squad's softball team from the summer they'd won the League championship.

A five-by-seven photo of his parents. He still called them, but not as often. They viewed his move here—and especially his job at Happy Tails—as a serious demotion. One that was beneath his skillset and one that wasn't needed because nothing that happened to those little girls had been Zane's fault. Not really.

But Zane didn't see it that way.

He moved the frame to the side and retrieved a metal box. He wasn't a slob by any stretch, but the box had remained untouched for a long while and dust covered the lid. His dust rag evidently stopped at Mom and Dad's photo.

He worked the keyring around in his hand until he found the small piece that would pop the box's lid. Inside, the familiar greeted him. His pistol and clip.

An extra box of rounds.

His cuffs.

Three photos.

One with the freckled face of his red-headed girlfriend who'd left him when he spiraled into depression. He'd not been able to read her. Taken by her good looks and what he thought was loyalty, he'd fallen for her hard, and her departure was part of the reason he'd put up with Florida's damp swelter. The Colorado cold reminded him of her. After all this time, he wasn't sure why he kept Zoe's picture.

He *did* know why he kept the other two photos in the box. Photos of the two missing, now dead, little girls. Zane had been misguided and misled through the investigation. He should have seen it. Someone should have seen it.

He left the pistol and rounds. Company policy—only badge-carrying officers can carry. And Zane obliged. He didn't think he deserved that privilege anymore.

He ran his fingers over the tiny faces of the two little girls from Denver then tucked them under the cartridge box.

He removed the cuffs and their small silver keys, and his girlfriend's snapshot, and locked the box and tucked it behind Mom and Dad.

He wound the cuff keys onto his keyring next to Lola's gate key and hung the ring and his cuffs on the entryway hook for his adventure tomorrow. Whatever *that* might be.

He shoved the photo of the redhead into the garbage disposal, turned on the cold water, and flipped the switch.

Zane watched the disposal chomp Zoe's likeness into tiny bits along with his dab of uneaten Fruit Loops.

"Yeah, Dwight. Thanks for calling me back." Zane continued to browse through Marla's merchandise. He'd chatted with the cashier who'd given him a little background. A lonely old gal and her lonely old husband had started the place a few years ago when their adult children moved away and took their grandchildren with them. They weren't doing too bad. A steady trickle of customers meandered through the tiny shop. "I'm gonna be a little late. Keep an eye on things for me."

"No worries. No issues so far. Meteor threw up all night, but her handler said things are looking better now."

"Good. Keep me updated." Zane ended the call and turned his attention toward a wall of sun hats. Bright blues, all various child sizes. And all with the same embroidered label as those found in the enclosures.

"Got any pink ones?"

The cashier shrugged. "You'd have to ask Marla when she comes in later. Someone bought them all out last week. A few blue ones too. Marla thought for a daycare or something."

Or something.

Zane took a blue one from the shelf. Ten bucks for a comparison piece wasn't too bad. He paid the cashier and stuffed the hat in his back pocket. He pulled the door open to leave when a bulletin board framed in bright yellow scrollwork caught his eye. Tacked to it, all over it in fact, were Happy Tails tickets. Free admission passes given out for special occasions or, like yesterday, in the event the zoo had to close or issue rainchecks.

Zane popped one off the board and handed it to the girl. "Where'd these come from?"

She shrugged again. "Same guy that bought the hats brought the tickets. Marla was tickled. She's been handing them out to all the kids."

"Did you see this guy?"

"No. I wasn't here that day." She handed the ticket back to him.

Zane looked up to the corners of the store for security cameras—something he would've done first thing four years ago, but working at Happy Tails had rubbed some of the sharpness away.

"Do you have security footage?"

"Only outside. Marla says they can't afford the cameras inside."

Zane stepped out and looked up where a single camera was

pointing down toward the door. He waved at the lens, then went back inside. "Do you keep the footage?"

Another shrug.

Zane's irritation grew. He'd rather deal with menopausal women than millennials. "Marla's phone number? Not the store's. Her personal one."

The cashier eyed him warily. "I'm not sure I should give that out. She'll be in in a few hours."

Zane's instinct was to reach in his back pocket for his badge, but all he felt was the round metal of his cuffs. His patience was coffee-filter thin, and he was about to pull out his cell to phone Warren when his phone vibrated in his hand. It was Dwight. Frantic.

"Got another lost kid, boss."

"And another hat? Blue?"

"How'd you know? In with Nellie. Good thing she's too slow to get to it. Michelle spotted it. Got her sitting with the mom now while the available staff combs the park. Called it in."

"Good work. I'll be there as soon as I can." Zane hung up and leaned over the counter, making some serious Detective-Zane-Frasier eye contact with the clerk. "I'm coming back later, that footage better be available. And Marla needs to answer some questions."

Zane grabbed all the Happy Tails tickets off the bulletin board, sending push pins all over the concrete floor, and stormed out of the boutique.

***

Zane sped the Jeep through the back gate of Happy Tails and was surprised to hear sirens as he made his way to Tella's exhibit. He was even more surprised to see the ambulance had pulled all the way into the park.

Two paramedics knelt on the pavement while others paced; a woman was crying.

Not good. Not good.

He jumped from the vehicle and pushed his way through the crowd. On the ground between the medical team was a little boy in a bright blue hat. His lips were a softer shade of blue. Ice cream melted out of its cone beside him on the hot asphalt.

"What happened here?"

Dwight reached him, out of breath, and pulled him aside. "Boy's allergic to peanuts. Cliff found him."

"Cliff. Again?"

Dwight nodded.

"Cliff give him the ice cream?"

Dwight nodded.

Zane took out the blue hat from his pocket. The price tag still hung from the brim. "Hat look like this?" Dwight pulled a similar— albeit muddy—hat from his own back pocket and nodded.

"What's going on here, Zane?"

Michelle approached the men. "I didn't sign up for this. Not for this." She'd been one of the frantic pacers near the boy.

"Where's the mom?" Zane asked.

Michelle pointed to the crying lady and Zane made his way to her. "Ma'am. Can you tell me what happened?" He did his best to aim her shoulders away from the boy on the ground.

All she could do was shake her head and mumble something about a free ticket. And that this wasn't supposed to happen. "It was a free ticket."

Slowly, the pieces started falling into place. Zane could see the setup and the payoff. But he couldn't figure the motive. Not quite.

Coughing from behind caused them both to spin and look toward the child. The little boy was sitting up with the help of the paramedic, pale and shaky, but breathing. The mother went hysterical all over again and collapsed to her knees next to her son, smothering him in kisses and hugs until the boy pushed her away for more air.

"I didn't sign up... I thought..." Michelle was mumbling behind Zane.

He faced her. He saw her face. Her concern. Concern he'd

mistaken yesterday for anxiety over the events in the gator exhibit. He felt a tug deep in his gut. A tug he remembered having dozens of times long ago before the missing girls' case. That tug indicating his radar was sharp and he was reading another human being with accuracy. Something he'd failed to practice with Zoe. Failed to practice with the perp in that case. But he wasn't going to fail with Michelle. "Maybe we need to head over to Command Central and you can tell me exactly what you *didn't* sign up to do."

"Wait, what?" Dwight tried to process Zane's firm tone. "What?"

"Let's all take a ride." Zane guided the pair to the Jeep and fired up the ignition.

Zane offered bottled water to Michelle and Dwight. Dwight downed his. Michelle never touched her bottle. She let it set on the table, dripping condensation in a small puddle. She'd cried from the time they got into the Jeep and was drying up the river now.

"Someone better start talking. 'Cause I got no idea what's happening," Dwight said as he stood to refill his bottle at the sink.

"How many more blue hats are out there today?"

Dwight's eyes got big and he glared at Michelle. "You *know?*"

Michelle took a deep breath and whispered "Four."

"Where?" Zane demanded.

She rattled off the enclosures.

Dwight slumped back and stared open-jawed at his trainee. "Why, Michelle?"

She shrugged a little. "We thought it would help. Help bring awareness. Help get more funds for security." She looked Zane straight in the face. "But I never, never wanted anyone to come to harm. We had no idea bout the boy's allergy. We thought..."

"Wait, you're a, you're a *Rightie?*" Dwight got up and paced.

Zane stood and put a firm hand on his shoulder. "You'd better walkie those enclosures now. And walk off the anger, man. Don't do anything stupid." Zane handed him the keys to the Jeep. "Help where you can. Keep the crews' safety first. No wrestling hats out of the lion's jaws."

"She's a friggin' *Rightie!*" Dwight stomped from the building, walkie in hand, already contacting PopPop's handler in the leopard enclosure.

Zane leaned against the wall near the window. The poor AC unit rattled and shook as it tried to battle the internal humidity. "You said 'we.' Does that include Cliff?" Zane hated to hear her reply because he already knew what the answer would be.

Everyone's grandfather. Easy for kids to trust. To be comforted by.

To take peanut-laden ice cream from.

"Do I need these?" Zane retrieved his cuffs from his back pocket and slid them across the table in front of Michelle. She shook her head. She'd given up. Ready to be done with the whole ordeal.

And Zane was glad. Last night he wasn't sure what he'd face today. This wasn't what he expected, but it was better than chasing a child predator through the park and having to cuff him to Lola's fence. Rightie fights, at least today's, consisted of more docile criminals. A misguided young woman and a slow, bored old man.

"Cliff part of the activists?"

"No. Not at first. He just liked us girls. Me and the girls at the gate. And we'd told him we could help maybe get him another crew member. Maybe working cameras. I had access to the exhibits. They had access to the guests and the free tickets. Cliff was, well—"

"Bored and lonely."

Michelle nodded, a fresh wave of tears cascaded down her cheeks and the group's feeble attempt at "helping Happy Tails" trickled out. The gate girls had given Cliff the packet of free tickets. He took the tickets to a touristy place—turned out to be Marla's—and gave her the tickets for her customers. He'd purchased a dozen hats in blues and pinks and then they waited. It was only a matter of time before someone who'd bought their child a hat also took advantage of the free zoo tickets—because who doesn't like free entertainment on vacation—and the gate would inform Michelle it was time to drop the hats while Cliff abandoned his duties for a moment to play dear old grandpa and offer a child—wearing the same color of hat as those tossed in with the animals—an ice cream, effectively luring the tot away from Mom.

"I didn't mean to get him in trouble. I wanted to stop it yesterday after Lola and Meteor…and watching that mom. But we didn't think we'd—"

"Get caught? Endanger young children? Nearly kill one of them? Induce strokes in their mothers?" Zane couldn't stop himself. "Endanger the very animals you people swear you're protecting?"

He snatched up the cuffs from the table and made another executive decision. "Know what? Maybe next time you really should *think*." He cuffed her hands behind her back and escorted her out of the building. He marched her through the park, openly for all to see, and right up to the front gate.

By the time they made the trek, both were out of breath and drenched in sweat. Dwight had called Warren who greeted Zane at the entrance. He'd already cuffed two of the other girls and Cliff was in the back of the squad car, lips puckered and tears brimming under his blue eyes.

"Good work, Detective." Warren said and Zane winced. "Why the face? What?"

"I *was* a detective. In Denver. I'm not anymore."

"Well, I meant it as a joke, but if you ever want to reinstate, we could use a good man." Warren nodded toward the zoo. "Get you out of this monkey business." He laughed at his own joke.

Dwight had come up on the pair and caught what Warren had said. His eyes were still as big as beach balls and he was still shaking in disbelief. He glanced in the back of the second patrol car, which now housed Michelle, who didn't look up from her lap.

"Guess she can kiss Mickey Mouse goodbye."

Zane laughed. "Yup." He shook Warren's hand.

"I mean it about the offer. Come by the station. We'll chat."

Zane nodded. "I'll think about it."

The officers took away their morning catch and Dwight and Zane looked toward the now-vacant ticket booths. A few visitors had lined up, waiting to gain entrance. Dwight went over and unlocked the windows, reaching in and retrieved free tickets for the dozen or so that had been standing for so long, watching the drama unfold. The guests were grateful and hurried through the gates.

"Did you mean that? That you'd think about the job offer?"

Zane walked with Dwight through the gates to the back of the ticket booths and entered the tiny ticket-taking cubicle together, each taking a seat where the Rightie girls had been just moments before. The air conditioning blasted cool, dry air. And the men relaxed a bit.

"Maybe." Zane fiddled with the printer, familiarizing himself with the setup so he and Dwight could man the front until the replacement staff could arrive.

Dwight's shoulders slumped. "Lola would miss your smiling face, Detective."

"Yeah, I bet she would." A few more guests purchased tickets and Dwight and Zane handled the transactions like pros.

"I'll probably stay," Zane said as he leaned back, allowing the AC to bathe him in cold.

Denver cold.

He wriggled the bright blue hat from his pocket and punched his fist into the middle to give the hat its shape back. He tossed it on top of Dwight's head. "But I'm moving Command Central to one of these cubicles."

Niche Market

In the quaint community of New Osgood, Mark Waterman runs an estate agency for some very specific clients. The contracts are iron-clad in this cutthroat market, but that doesn't mean that greediness will be tolerated.

Mark Waterman slid two brochures and two contracts into his burgundy eelskin case, a gift from his last client. He ran his hands over the smooth leather and took a deep, satisfying breath. The latest prospects, a husband and wife from New York City, contacted him last night for his services. He had the perfect property lined up for them—a quiet, white bungalow two blocks from his own home on the edge of New Osgood, population eight hundred ninety-seven. A majority of that population Mark and his predecessor had expertly placed within the community.

He grabbed his keys from the entryway table and decided to walk to the showing. The day was bright and beautiful, no humidity, light cloud cover. He shrugged his shoulders to straighten his jacket and reached up with his free hand to straighten his tie. The heels of his vintage Berlutis clacked on the sidewalk. He waved at a passerby, one of his satisfied clients, and tried to clear his mind for his meeting.

Joel and Joyce Sorrell contacted Mark three weeks ago. He told them as soon as a spot became available, he'd let them know. The previous owners passed away four days after his initial contact with the Sorrells. Mark had snatched up the property with his own capital, earmarked for such occurrences in New Osgood, and sent notice to the couple. They were ecstatic.

Mark caught the faint scent of honeysuckle wafting from Mrs. Olson's side yard. She was on her knees in the dirt, digging and tending to her roses. Her one-third acre lot was the brightest for several streets. Everyone thought she had the greenest thumb in the state. Mark knew better, though. Mrs. Olson's late husband had hired Mark's mentor as his realtor two decades ago under a single contract. According to the file, Barry Olson married Nancy for cover and her cooking.

"Afternoon, Mrs. Olson!" He waved to her.

"Same to you, Mr. Waterman!"

"How are you feeling these days?"

"Oh, a bit slower, a bit slower. But I guess that's to be expected with old age." She reached around and massaged her back.

"I guess it is." Mark chuckled politely, Mrs. Olson turned to her roses, and he continued one more block down the peaceful street.

He had two more clients on the wait list, and only one property to close on this week. Mrs. Olson's would probably be the next spot to open, but the old gal clung to life like it meant something.

He climbed the four stone steps to the bungalow's front porch. The Sorrells hadn't arrived yet, so he took a seat on the porch swing, listening as the loose ends of the chains clanked against the supports. He spread his arms out across the back of the swing, tilted his head back and closed his eyes. What a perfect day.

He tried to remember his first sale. His mentor explained to him some twenty years ago that niche markets like theirs took time and patience to cultivate. Mark almost quit a couple of times under the stress of it all, but quitting meant more than a simple career change. It meant changing one's whole identity.

And niche markets like theirs also meant one never retired. As long as there is breath, there is the job.

He heard a car pull up and saw his clients eyeing the place through the rolled-down windows of their Mercedes.

"Good day, Mr. and Mrs. Sorrell!" This part he hated. The initial face-to-face. There are some things they couldn't teach in realtor school. Either you relate to people or you don't. Mark didn't. Mark faked graciousness and generosity and understanding every day. Then he retreated to his own two-story sanctuary with his solitary hobbies, filling his emotional and mental cup for the next day's duties.

The good-looking couple exited the car and stood on the side-walk, taking in the view of the street and their potential new home. The blue Armani gave the gentleman an air of importance and intim-idation. The lady wore a white sundress that reached her ankles. She pulled her sunglasses to the top of her head and shielded her eyes as she inspected the house.

Mark unlocked the front door and met them at the bottom of the steps. He stuck his hand out, expecting a firm handshake from Joel. He wasn't disappointed. To Joyce he held out his hand palm-up. She placed her hand in his and he lifted it to his lips and kissed her in greeting. She blushed a little, which surprised him, given their profile.

Or she was as good at faking niceties as Mark was.

"Would you like a moment to inspect the outside, or shall we begin the tour?"

"Let's go in, if you don't mind," Joel said.

"After you." He stepped into the grass so the couple could go ahead. Mark never turned his back on new clients.

The couple held hands as they crossed the porch and entered the front door. Mark was careful to keep his eyes on the back of their heads instead of where he'd like to look—at Joyce's slender silhouette beneath her thin frock. That's how Mark had inherited the New Osgood territory. His mentor had made the mistake of allowing his eyes to linger a bit too long on the frame of Grant Cook's wife. And that was that.

He crossed the threshold into the front room. "I'd be happy to point out specifics, if you'd like. Or I can wait in the kitchen for you with some printed information and allow you to explore on your own."

Joyce smiled at him and adjusted the sunglasses on top of her blonde head. Joel eyed the room and said, "I think we'll be fine. If we have questions, we'll ask." They continued to hold hands as they explored the house. Mark wondered how much of that was genuine affection or for display.

"Sure thing." Mark moved to the kitchen and began spreading out paperwork for the couple to inspect. He had two contracts for this case. He laid the trifold brochures on top of the paperwork. And on top of it all, he placed two brand new Visconti fountain pens. An ebony limited edition with platinum nib for the gentleman, and a gold-nibbed peach beauty for the lady.

Most couples signed one contract because, usually, one of the pair had no clue whom they'd married, and that came with an extra delicate dance during the showing and utmost confidentiality between Mark and the lead buyer. This was only the fourth time in all his years that a pair needed individual contracts. That meant they knew.

"Well, what do you think?" Mark asked as the couple came into the kitchen.

Joyce looked disappointed. "It's quaint. Not quite what I expected for the money."

"This is as good as it gets, dear. We can't be too fussy." Joel ran his finger across the countertop.

"Is there anything else in the area that is a little more... well, modern?" Joyce opened a cupboard above the stove.

Mark got this question a lot. His clients were accustomed to having the best of the best. With a relocation and a slower-paced lifestyle, sometimes they had a hard time adjusting. On the other hand, those same adjustment issues often led to vacant properties. "This is the only home in New Osgood that's move-in ready at the moment. I have one in closing now, but it's smaller and older by a decade."

He thought about mentioning Mrs. Olson's place, but held his tongue. He had too many details to work out before he could offer that property.

"I just don't know. I was hoping for something more grand." Joyce stood with a hand on her hip and tucked a curl of blonde hair behind her ear with the other.

Mark hesitated, then said, "I could put you in touch with the realtor over in Dover Junction, a sister community to ours, but that's out of state quite a ways. I'm not sure what his fee is these days, either." He only offered this because he could sense Joyce was going to be high maintenance.

"No, no. We need to be a little closer to the city for our work. That won't do," Joel said.

Joyce elbowed him in the ribs and whispered, "Ask him."

He rolled his eyes and said, "On the way down the street, we noticed a home about a block back. The one with all the roses. Is that one available?"

"If all the houses are this old, the least we could do is find one with a beautiful yard."

Mark nodded. He knew he should have dealt with Mrs. Olson months ago. "I know the property. The elderly lady there takes good care of it."

Joel put both hands in his pockets, and in doing so, he exposed the Glock pistol tucked in his waist band. "How much extra to make it available, say, by the end of the week?"

"Well, there's the contracts that have to be redone and the–"

"Joel, please." Joyce puckered her bottom lip and leaned into his chest. He looked perturbed, but put an arm around her.

"I was led to believe you're the best realtor in this business, Mr. Waterman. Make it happen. No price is too steep for a little peace and quiet on the home front." Joyce elbowed him in the ribs again.

Mark smiled and nodded. He packed away the pens and paperwork and said, "I'll make it happen. You'll hear from me soon."

Another handshake to the gentleman. Another courtesy kiss to the lady's hand. Mark locked up the empty bungalow, saw the Sorrells to their car, and walked the two blocks home. He had details to work out.

Mark traded his suit jacket and tie for a t-shirt and sweats, but not before he fastened the concealed carry wrap around his midsection. He slid open the cylinder and spun it twice, checking for debris and snug ammo placement. He tucked the revolver into the pouch on the wrap, placed his dress shoes on the closet shelf and laced up his runners. After a quick microwave dinner, he headed back down the street toward the bungalow, passing Mrs. Olson's home.

He could see the flicker of the TV through the lacy sheers blowing in the breeze. The evening air was crisp and fresh. Night would fall in another hour or so. He passed the empty bungalow, which would now house one Mr. Samuel Twain, no doubt an alias. Mark's payday would be massive this week. He dreamed of ways to spend the cash. Or to invest it.

He'd already sunk loads of cash into his own abode. Newly renovated and updated rooms and appliances. The best of the best.

He rounded the block near the police station—another one of Mark's investments in the town that was going very well. For the niche market to thrive, one had to have a solid, hand-picked police presence. Mark smiled. His mentor had taught him well.

He continued to run until he worked up a sweat, and timed it so that he'd be back to his block at night fall. It really was a beautiful night. The lightning bugs floated from the well-manicured lawns like miniature hot air balloons. Crickets provided the background music.

A few more blocks to go.

Maybe a vacation to the city. Stay at the St. Regis, catch a ferry out to Liberty Island for an afternoon. Visit Times Square. He'd made his decision and smiled. He was close enough now to smell the honeysuckle.

He knocked on Mrs. Olson's front door. He could hear the television in the background.

The old lady opened the door slowly and peeked her head out. "Oh, it's you, Mr. Waterman. Is everything okay?"

"Yes ma'am. I was wondering if I could speak to you for a moment. It's about your roses."

"If you won't mind waiting. I'm in my nightgown. Just a moment." She shut the door gently, and for anyone passing on the street who cared to look in the direction of the front porch, it appeared he was waiting patiently. But Mark now felt the weight of the holster and the gun against his skin. The anticipation of the event created more adrenaline and sweat than his jog had.

"Okay, I'm ready for you. Come on in." She wore a lavender bath robe and carried a pitcher of lemonade. Two tall glasses with ice cubes waited on the coffee table. She showed him to the sofa and turned off the TV.

"Mrs. Olson – Nancy. Can I call you Nancy?"

"If I can call you Mark." She grinned and handed him a sweaty glass of ice cold sweetness. She stood in front of him and watched as he took a long sip and held the glass in his lap. The cold dripping from the glass onto his legs helped him to focus.

"I was wondering how long you've been tending those roses, Nancy. If I remember correctly, they were planted before you and Barry married." He took another sip.

"Let's cut this out, shall we, Mr. Waterman?" She poured herself a glass and drank half of it before setting it on the coffee table. She straightened herself and pulled a Ruger from her robe and aimed it at Mark's head. "I've been wondering when you would come by to discuss more than the weather."

Mark fumbled the glass, dumping lemonade and ice cubes onto his crotch.

"Stay seated, please, Mr. Waterman. Mark. Barry warned me on his deathbed about this day. About the contract he signed."

"Now, Mrs. Olson, let's have a rational discussion." Mark put his arms up, adrenaline pumping. He could probably lunge and take her down and only suffer a flesh wound if she managed to get a shot off.

"We *are* having a rational discussion." She was calm, as steady as any seasoned criminal client Mark had ever worked with. "You can't have my home. I didn't sign the contract. Barry did."

"That's not how it works, Mrs. Olson." Mark stood and reached for his piece.

It was the last thing Mark Waterman did.

On a beautiful summer morning two weeks later, Mr. and Mrs. Sorrell took a jog down the block from their home in New Osgood. They paused to greet sweet old Mrs. Olson tending her roses.

"Good morning, Nancy!"

Nancy stood and brushed the dirt from her knees and hands. "Good morning!"

"Looks like you have a new addition to your rose garden," Joel said.

She smiled and admired her freshly cultivated patch with new white roses. "How are you enjoying the old Waterman place, Joyce?"

"It's grand. Just grand." And the couple continued their jog.

LANDMARKS

Former Navy SEAL Jackson Renalt has been thrust into a position he never wanted and forced to patrol a hometown he never really knew. Disoriented by life's twists and turns and those of the patchwork county roads, Jackson finds his footing and forges new landmarks... with a little help from the locals.

Sheriff Jackson Renalt unhooked the metal-pronged star from his jeans pocket and placed it in the front passenger seat of the rusty blue Chevy Silverado next to the paper bag of white powdered doughnuts and quart of chocolate milk. The truck had been retrofitted in true redneck style just months ago with handcuff holds, bars, and spit glass. The spit glass needed a good spit-shine and the bars could do with some tightening down.

No one could have been prepared for the fallout once he'd gotten back from Iraq. No one. Not even a SEAL. So the rednecks were happy to help the Sheriff keep their county clean and safe from scum like Willie Daniel Suede, and the Landry boys helped him make do with his daddy's truck.

'Cause if anyone was gonna cause a ruckus, it'd be the good 'ol Landry boys.

But not Willie Daniel Suede, by god.

Jackson had trained with an elite squad straight out of high school for what he thought would be overseas issues. Or border patrol. Or, well, anything other than cleaning up home-grown challenges in his dying and decrepit home county of Collins.

He didn't want to be anywhere near his home county of Collins, save for those obligatory Christmas visits or Mother's Days when, if he were state-side, he'd make an appearance and fill the emotional cups of his folks and a few others in the town.

He unholstered his gun and tossed it rather irreverently into the seat with the badge as he climbed into the truck. The fraying, stained seat fabric caught on his jeans, but he slid past, making the rip worse and placed his bald head against the steering wheel and breathed. He'd have to collect the badge and gun and wear them appropriately when he got to the prisoner pickup. But for now, they could sit in time out. And wait.

Sheriff Jackson Renalt.

Not a title that he'd dreamed of having in a million years.

Sheriffs are supposed to win elections.

Sheriffs are supposed to rise through the ranks after police academy and shoulder rubbing and politic-ing.

Sheriffs are supposed to know the roads in their jurisdiction like the veins running on their own hands. Life and blood in the power of direction and fast navigations.

Sheriffs aren't supposed to be dubbed Leader With A Gun simply because everyone else is dead or dying.

And Sheriffs definitely aren't supposed to use roadkill as landmarks for right turns.

He sat upright, not bothering with a seatbelt, and twisted the key in the ignition. At least it wasn't raining yet, and he'd be able to make out his landmarks on the way to the Burris's. He left his sunglasses on the dashboard. The gray overcast skies were easy on the eyes, even if the August humidity was about to swallow him whole.

His dad's old Chevy shook alive and he pointed the nose toward the country road away from his parents' bungalow on the corner of Chester and Cherry and turned right out of the gravel drive. He passed a dozen other bungalows of the same shape and size as he left the burg, now empty or soon would be.

The fireplace mantel in his folks' home supported his baby and childhood photos, all in mismatched frames. His trophies from T-Ball and Little league collected dust on one corner. The Academy's awards stacked and framed on the other. Just him. No siblings. His folks' pride and joy and one and only.

As he drove out of Collinsburg he wondered how many other mantels in the town were covered with dust and memories. How many other families abandoned the country for safety in numbers or at least access to better health care and a constant supply chain of toilet paper, denture cream, and antennae television.

Not to mention access to more like Jackson. More officers keeping watch. More Guard patrolling. Keeping the evils such as Willie Daniel Suede at bay.

But none of those other mantel-dwelling sons and daughters Jackson grew up with was a son of a son of a son of the local sheriff.

The Renalts ruled this simple country area with its simple kindly populous with kindness and fairness for generations. So Jackson had been tagged Man With A Gun and carried the torch, no matter if he wanted it or not. No matter if the pronged sheriff's badge cut into his midsection every time he bent. And he hated shirts with pockets.

Jackson lived in his SEAL t-shirts, and there's no good place to hang a rural county badge on a Navy SEAL t-shirt.

He reached the edge of the town and started using landmarks. Right at the red leaning barn that no longer housed Dwight's milk cows. Left at the stop sign that leaned left after one of the Burris's drunk-drove their pickup into the ditch. Another left five or so miles down at the T guarded by the oak tree taller and wider than any other. The oak where kids came as soon as they could drive to carve initials into the trunk and make out under—or in—the branches. He didn't turn left right away. He killed the air conditioner and rolled down the windows and put the truck in park, allowing the cawing crows and the rumble of the engine to drown the stress-induced ringing in his ears.

His initials were on that trunk somewhere.

JR and LT roped in a heart. Lillian Thomas became Lillian Rogers—not Renalt—and that decision—her decision—had sealed Jackson's decision to join the military. Start over.

She was the reason he'd come back though. The real reason. Not to be sheriff. Not to answer the pleas of a terrified town. Not even because of his parents, though he would've come for them. Out of respect.

But really, what made pinning the star to his jeans worth the trouble was Lillian.

Lillian. And her little girl.

His life had been one series of disorienting moves after another. Despite his training, he felt ungrounded and way out of his depths even on his home turf. Lillian had a lot to do with that.

He guessed he'd lost his landmarks.

And what Willie did to them. To his parents. To so many others in one evil rampage was beyond comprehension. Justice would be served, Jackson would see to it. He was the sheriff, after all. And in a few moments, Willie Daniel Suede would be handcuffed in the back seat of the Chevy behind the spit glass and bars and hauled four counties over where they finally had staff and jail space to hold him until he could be sentenced.

He'd get life. No doubt.

Likely get the death penalty. No lawyer wanted this case.

No jail wanted to house him, either. Especially not the smaller establishments in the rural counties.

And the only thing the bastard ever wanted to eat was white powdered doughnuts and chocolate milk. Three meals a day. Even joked through yellowed and crooked teeth as he clung to the bars in the Burris's barn that he'd request white powered doughnuts and chocolate milk as his last meal, should the good state decide to lay him to rest.

Lay him to rest.

Rest wouldn't be justice.

Put him to death. That sounded better.

More bile encroached as he stifled the urge to put a fist through the bag of doughnuts and dump the milk out the window. Let the crows have a little variety in their hydration options.

Jackson turned left and started watching for that final landmark, hoping it would be there. Hoping the vultures and buzzards and Willie Daniel Suedes of the animal kingdom had left the deer at the corner of this road and the nearly invisible gravel one he needed to turn right on.

The roads out this far were either marked poorly, not marked, or the rednecks had stolen what markers there were to use the metal poles and aluminum signage in some homegrown project. His stomach turned and bile built in the back of his throat as it had done a half dozen times a day since this all started.

He slowed the truck, scanning, looking.

And there it was.

The doe his deputy sheriff had nailed with the other pickup on the way to relieve Jackson of guard duty when the Willie thing began. Poor thing didn't stand a chance, and Spencer had done right by her and put her down with his pistol. The scavengers were working though, reclaiming nature, so to speak. By this time next week, her mound of flesh would be a pile of bones the same dusky shade as the drying weeds and gravel and would no longer serve as such as stark signpost.

He turned right. Thankful that his part in this nightmare was nearly done. Let justice be served and move on.

The country roads in Collins County were patchwork-quilt straight. Serving to border corn and soybeans and hay fields all laid out in various squares and rectangles. And without the landmarks, one square began to look like the next and the next. His dad and granddad had these roads etched into their brains.

But depending on GPS and phone-assisted mapping, Jackson had been spoiled and never needed to learn the lay of the land.

Until now. Until the towers went dark or disabled in this part and landlines and basic cell functions were all that was left. His one deputy and he had one police radio set. And that's about it. Poor 'ol Spencer needed relieved after a twenty-four-hour stretch guarding Willie out at the Burris's place. Way out at the Burris's place.

So far out and so far away with so few people that no communication provider even cared to service the towers. The smart folks left a year ago and the next-smarter group left once Willie unleashed terror on Collins County and Jackson had been called in to carry a gun and hunt the murder-spree demon.

No GPS and no "Alexa, please guide me to Fulbright road."

Until the last wave of looters from the city came and torched the tiny police station, rendering the jail inoperable and creating the need for more creative prisoner housing, especially for the likes of Willie Daniel Suede.

So the Burris's place—all of them dead or gone or in some other county's jail—was the next best option. Because the Burisses specialized in housing all manner of wildlife in their barn. From the run-of-the-mill cows and horses to the more, well, extreme.

A tiger cub that PETA confiscated once they found out.

A collection of rattlesnakes that the boys thought they could raise for eggs.

A bear stolen from a drive-through circus—and thus the redneck-built triple-reinforced steel cage with lock. Those idiots left the gate unlocked, though, and Jackson's dad and his deputies back in the day literally went on a bear hunt. Locked the Burrisses in their own cage —all four boys, well, adults, but children nonetheless—until the bear was found and rehomed with the circus.

The neighbors a few miles over thought for sure the Burris gang had procured a gator or a crocodile or some other such water monster on their Florida trip and put the thing loose in the pond that sat next to the bear barn on the Burris's property. After what Jackson's grandfather and father had told and retold over the years, Jackson wouldn't put it past them.

The murky pond, about half the size of a football field and likely three times as deep, came up on his right. The cattails and overgrowth of algae would provide any crocodile or contraband serpent perfect cover. Jackson slowed and pulled the pickup into a no-longer-gravel lane, dust flying up in tiny tornados around the tires and layering the windshield with a fine coating of dingy brown. Jackson coughed and wished he'd remembered about the dirt. He'd have rolled up the windows.

The house, a two-story typical farmhouse, was overgrown with late-summer ivy, green and healthy, covering last year's late summer ivy dead and brown. Some of the second story windows were completely engulfed in vegetation.

Spencer's squad car was parked by the barn entrance. The green metal structure had been the Burris's pride and joy and the upkeep reflected it. Fresh white gravel, at least fresh as of last year, had been laid around the walls and along the parking areas. Three bay doors were closed and locked tight. Those doors would allow entrance of combines, planters, and a circus train, if need be.

Regular humans, the sheriff, deputy and prisoner kind, entered through a reinforced steel door, deadbolted and watched over by a security camera. Though Jackson and Spencer hadn't bothered with the camera. They were the only ones who knew where Willie Daniel Suede was kept. That was by design given the high profile of the case.

Jackson shook his head. He grabbed his gun, badge and the villain's lunch. He stretched for a moment to clear out the stress knots and looked back toward the pond. Movement caught his eyes, cattails swaying when there was no wind. Swaying ferociously. Like somethin' big was out there. Then ripples.

He'd been fishing enough with his daddy to know the way the water breaks when pond fish like bluegill or bass surface toward the top. That was not a bluegill or a bass.

Likely not a snake, either. Burris Boys always knew how to keep the local law enforcement busy—or at bay. He'd have to deal with the pond monster later. Another more evil creature awaited him in the barn.

He knocked on the steel door and was relieved when Spencer answered. It wasn't ideal, keeping someone like Willie in the middle of nowhere with only one guard, but the bear cage was substantial and they really had no other choice.

Inside, where most of the barns in these parts had gravel or dirt floors, this building had poured concrete, smooth and sectioned off in perfect squares. Cages of all sorts and containers of others lined the walls. LED bulbs hung in nice neat rows above. Cables for the security system crisscrossed this way and that, their ends disappearing in a row of monitors hung in the far corner.

The illegal critter world must've been lucrative even in these rural parts.

More likely the Burris Boys had found other ways to supplement and diversify their income.

"More doughnuts?"

Jackson nodded and handed Spencer the sweets and milk.

"You're too good to him, Jackson." Spencer turned to face the bear cage. "Lucky day, scumbag. Yet one more special order. Eat up." Spencer banged on the bars to get Willie's attention. The convict rose from his cot in the corner and grinned as Spencer shoved the food between the bars and let the doughnut sack and plastic milk container fall to the cement.

As Willie dug into the noontime breakfast menu, Spencer gave Jackson a run-of-the-mill rundown of the last 24 hours. Willie ate the previous offerings of powdered sugar and chocolate. Willie slept. Willie taunted. Willie claims he'll live on even if the state does put him to sleep. "He's calling himself the Infamous Willie Suede. The Collinsburg Killer."

"He named himself." Jackson leaned against the bars. Close enough to hear the devil swallow chocolate milk. Close enough to smell the powdered sugar mixed with body odor and the stench emanating from the five-gallon plastic bucket latrine in the far corner of the bear cage.

At this point in their makeshift shift change, Spencer would hold Willie at gunpoint while Jackson donned gloves and switched out the bucket. No need today. Today, Willie's white dusty palms would be handcuffed and the beast slapped into the back of Jackson's truck, tied down, and Jackson would transport him to his trial. Willie would swap out his sweatpants and Pioneer seed t-shirt for a bright orange jumpsuit.

"He doesn't deserve a trial, Jackson."

"That's not up to us."

"He robbed this town of what little they had left."

Willie grinned, wiping his chocolate milk moustache from his stubble onto his shirt sleeve. "That'd be me. The Infamous Willie—"

Jackson drew his gun, cocked it, and raked it against the bars. Willie stopped talking, but he didn't stop grinning.

"He took everything from you, Jacks."

It's not like Jackson hadn't thought about it. Thought about ending the need for a trial altogether. But he was an officer. A soldier. Trained and bound by duty to allow the system to do its thing.

"Well, have it your way, choir boy. Let's get this over with."

Spencer tossed Jackson the keys.

And missed. The keys landed in the cage with the killer bear and his chocolate milk.

Jackson and Spencer both drew on Willie.

"Well now, ain't this a fine turn of events. Fine indeed." Willie strode the four steps it took to reach the gate key. He slid his index finger into the keyring and twirled and grinned. Flashes of yellow teeth mixed with flashes of silver metal from the spinning key.

"Throw it out here, Willie," Spencer said.

"Nah. Don't think I will." Willie took a seat on his cot, still spinning the key.

"Willie, come on now. Let's get this over with. Don't you want a real toilet? Aren't you tired of pissing in a bucket?"

"Well, maybe." Willie looked at his latrine. "Or maybe I'm just right glad to have those powdered doughnuts. And that fine, smooth choco-milk." He paused and stared at Jackson straight in the face. "Smooth as that lass of yours...What was her name? Linda? Layla? Oh, I remember." He licked his lips and stood. "Smooth as the skin on Miss Lillian Rogers."

"You son-of-a—"

Willie leapt to his feet and dropped the keys in the latrine bucket. "I ain't goin' nowhere. And you ain't getting in here."

Jackson's head spun. He wanted to believe the taunting didn't bother him. But it did. What that monster did to his parents. Did to Lillian and her little girl. More bile bubbled up, but he forced it down, not wanting to give Willie the satisfaction of seeing him vomit.

"Spencer."

"Yeah boss."

"You can leave now."

Spencer lowered his gun a few inches. "You sure boss?"

"Can I trust you?" Beads of sweat formed at Jackson's brow line.

He hated that. Hated the fact that his SEAL t-shirt was soaking through, too.

"He killed my neighbors. Slaughtered them in their beds, Jacks. For that, I'd give ya backup for whatever your plan is."

"No. I do this alone."

"You're the boss." Spencer holstered his weapon and left the barn.

"Now you can't go killin' prisoners and getting away with it. A pretty boy like you'd not fair well in prison. Bein' a cop and all."

Jackson heard Spencer's squad car rev and the fine white gravel pop against the metal frame. "Now, wait, there sheriff. Hey Spencer!" Willie started for the bucket. Likely gonna fish out his keys and make a deal.

Jackson didn't let him get that far. He stood at an angle, aimed and fired at the locking mechanism on the cage. Splinters of metal and yellow sparks flew in all directions. Willie dropped to the ground and put his hands on his head. A good little boy.

"Get up. Keep your hands up. Get out here. And don't think I won't shoot." Jackson fired a second round into the roof of the barn.

Willie, wide-eyed, did what he was told and the pair walked outside. "Now, Sheriff. Jackson. How you think you gonna get me cuffed and into that there truck of yours?"

"I'm not gonna cuff you. I'm gonna make a deal with you."

"Let's make a deal. What a great day."

"You swim? The great and mighty Infamous Willie Suede. Do you swim?"

"Mighty fine swimmer. Thought about being an Olympian. Probably would've given Mikey Phelps a good run."

"Good. You swim across that pond. You can go free. Go into Collinsburg and loot the minimart and eat all the doughnuts you want."

"That's it?"

"That's it."

"You'll shoot me in the back."

"I'd not shoot an unarmed man. Unless you threaten me."

"Nah. I've done enough to you. Takin' your momma and your dadda and your precious Lillian and her bitty angel—"

Jackson fired another round into the gravel, spraying both their feet with shards of rocks.

"Okay, okay. I'll swim."

They walked across the crispy grass. The coming rain would wash away the dust from the blades and tomorrow they'd stand a little straighter. A little greener.

Willie yacked all the way to the pond. "Want I should take off my clothes."

"Nope. Shoes and all."

They reached the cattails. The ones that had been smashed down a half hour ago.

"Looks mighty nasty."

"Nasty shouldn't bother you."

"It doesn't."

"Swim. Now."

Thunder rolled in the distance. The humidity was increasing by the minute. The clouds couldn't handle the moisture load much longer and started to drip into the pond creating concentric circles all along the water.

Willie took a step in. Then another. He was up to his shins. "Keep goin."

"Now look, I think there's something in here."

"Turtles. And bluegill. Maybe a snake. But aren't reptiles just up your alley?"

Willie grinned back at Jackson. "I can smell freedom ringing now." He poised his arms over his head in Olympic dive style and jumped out into the pond. He rolled over on his back and back paddled. He was in the middle of the pond.

Come on. Come on. Jackson kept his gun trained on the murderer.

Come on, Burris Boys. Don't fail me now.

Then it happened.

Teeth and claws and screams and blood. Thunder and a downpour.

One monster rolled the other until the water churned dark despite the murk.

And the Infamous Willie Daniel Suede, the Collinsburg Killer, met his match and a hefty dose of justice in a redneck's pond in the middle of nowhere Collins county.

Jackson thought about firing his weapon at the gator. Or croc. He wasn't sure which. But he'd deal with that another time. He may need that gator as an alibi for when that sneaky murderer escaped police custody and took off running for the pond.

Jackson watched until the water went still except for those little concentric circles from the rain. Perfect little doughnut rings all over the water's surface.

He got back in his truck, tossed the badge and the gun into the seat next to him. He started the engine and headed back to Collinsburg, following his landmarks before the buzzards came for the rest of the roadkill.

CREAM AND MERINGUE

Shaw and Sharon are the perfect couple. Hand-in-glove, peas in a pod, birds of a feather.
Inseparable. But after a discovery at his forensics lab, Shaw begins to wonder just how much alike they really are—and if Sharon really is as sweet as Meringue...

S haw Wycliff was a lab geek in every sense of the word—to the point of dreading the times when his division of the forensic building was closed and he was forced to shut down the 3D printer, hang up his lab coat, and let his hands go naked for seventy-two-hour weekend stretches.

That is until he met his one true. His Sharon.

He parked in the driveway of their bungalow with its hunter green siding. Soon, the shrubbery in the landscaping would bush out and swallow the front windows. The locust trees in the yard were starting to fragrance the air with spring sweetness. Daffodils danced along the sidewalk, although sparsely because neither he nor Sharon cared much about home upkeep, much to the chagrin of their suburban neighbors.

His wife, fifteen years ago and every day since, had been correct in choosing the 'burbs for their landing pad. As singles, they'd preferred apartment life close to the action of their jobs, but together, they needed a hidey-hole of sorts to let the rest of the world do what it will and to be at peace. The air here remained clear and crisp even in the humid summers—and that alone made the commute worth it. Today the breeze carried the season's first hint of freshly cut grass, the hum of lawnmowers, and the occasional squeal of a child who'd been boxed in a wintery cage far too long.

Her car was already in the drive. He laid one hand on the hood. The slightest bit of warmth radiated from the engine. He put his other hand on the car and allowed the gentle heat to ease his aching fingers. He'd been testing the fractures and forces of various objects in the lab today. His 3D printer made replicas of possible murder weapons from cold case files, and his job was to test them out. Smash that object into that skull model. Slam that glass shard into that rib cage rendering. Gripping. Hitting. Then inputting raw data into the computer and let that monster of a mainframe calculate and compare and tally to root out monsters from the past.

When the engine's heat lost its effect, he moved on to the front door. She'd not been home too long. Probably cooking dinner. Normally, the sight of her car next to his would lift his soul from whatever grim discovery he'd made in the lab that day, or lift his soul higher if work was business as usual.

But today he wondered where'd she'd been and who she'd seen. Today he wondered if he knew her at all. But as he opened the front door and the baking lasagna caused his taste buds to water more ferociously than Pavlov's dogs, some of his doubts softened, the hole in his stomach betraying his resolve for home-cooked Italian.

"Hey, Peaches. Be there in just a minute," Sharon called from around the kitchen. She called him her Peaches 'N Cream. Because he was always sweet. All the time. Even when her goat of a father threatened to shoot him dead if he didn't stop dating her. Even when at the funeral everyone thought Shaw had something to do with the old man's demise so he could up and marry Sharon.

Even when they emerged from the wedding chapel, and her delirious uncle's gunshots rang above their heads. Real gunfire landed the uncle in jail and then the vulgarity-spewing aunt dropped dead of a heart attack, landing her six feet in the ground next to Sharon's dad.

Though Shaw got blamed for it all, Sharon never questioned his unwavering kindness and inability to never hurt another living soul.

Even when Sharon had insisted—*insisted*—that the cockatoo statue not be abandoned in her childhood home, he remained altogether benevolent despite internal annoyance over the bird.

Shaw prided himself on the way he treated her. Respectful. Considerate. Once, she'd accused him of using a thesaurus and acting out every adjective he could find which was, well, nice. He'd smiled and kissed her and told her she was worth every positively connotated word in the book. She'd melted into his arms and soaked up the moment. After her upbringing, as far as affection goes, she was a dry sponge.

Shaw was mostly a recluse, preferring to hide in the basement behind his lab coat and gloved hands and face shield. He was known around the building as the nice guy in the cold case room—even when someone higher up the food chain became difficult to deal with, Shaw remained polite. Polite makes people go away faster.

Usually.

And generally staying away from people mostly kept him sweet.

Mostly.

Either that or the opportunity to smash and hit and swing at human body dummies all day long. That can also release lots of tension.

Sharon was his Lemon Meringue. A little tangy with a dollop of sugar—the way he liked her. She, too, wore protective gear every day and worked in the same field, but more public facing. She needed strong tang to deal with the outside world and the horrors that crime scenes dealt and the multiple personalities that made up their police force.

She'd needed nothing but tang to survive her family. And he leaned heavily on her when his own family became victims of rogue violence during the time they were dating. Shaw was never close to his parents, but the hold they had on him and the way they took advantage of his kindness, Sharon couldn't tolerate. "It's another form of abuse. You just don't have bruises or scars to show someone."

She was right. He'd drop everything he was doing to do their bidding. No matter what else was going on.

Sharon told him his parents were too needy.

She was right. The one time he tried to go against them, even as an adult, his dad went on a rampage and keyed Shaw's very first car— a little Escort he'd saved for months and months to buy. "It's just the beginning. You've got to get away. Your parents just started a lot later than mine did."

And after their untimely deaths, Shaw realized how right she was —as always. As mortifying as the whole ordeal was, their deaths freed him to help her. Even if Sharon hadn't been in his life, their deaths would've freed him to actually have a life.

Sharon said that's why she chose forensics—to help catch killers. And that's likely why Shaw went into cold cases. To help catch killers. Or, in Sharon's family's case, to clear the innocent of damning charges.

As the years went on, though, despite her crime scene work, Sharon's sweet, soft Meringue side bubbled to the top more and more. Shaw wondered what her personality would be like if she'd been raised by kind folks instead of the abusive pair fate dealt her.

When it was just the two of them, Shaw and Sharon, alone in their bungalow surrounded by their books and classic movies and vintage Atari systems, they were, well, sweet. Even through snarky board game battles or "fights" about the true origin of a word during Scrabble, or whose turn it was to empty the dishwasher. To each other, they remained Cream and Meringue.

Sharon called out a few more niceties from the kitchen. He'd yet to see her today, a before-dawn phone call tore her from their bed and off to a crime scene before he'd even hit the shower. They texted back and forth some, but not much. When she was at an active crime scene, her phone stayed in the car.

But as Shaw stood near the built-in bookcase of their tidy bungalow and ran his fingers over her marble cockatoo mounted on its purple amethyst base, feeling the bird's curves and creases, feeling the crystal points of the base, Shaw began to wonder if his wife's lemon was tangier than he'd known.

Altogether sour, really.

"You okay, babe? I didn't hear if you answered me." She poked her head around the corner, her black locks pulled into a messy bun on top of her head.

Shaw smiled, sweetly. "That sounds great. Just had a day, sweetheart." He hoped the strain in his voice didn't give away how truly horrified he was.

"Oh, no. I'm so sorry. Made a strawberry pie, too. For later." She winked. She had a smudge of flour across her olive-toned cheek. She was wearing that dumb apron he thought so cute. Still did. She'd dripped tomato sauce—or maybe it was strawberries—down the front. Underneath, she wore a short-sleeved t-shirt and jeans. She'd showered since she'd been home. Even over all the baking, he could smell her soap. Fresh and clean.

She went back to the kitchen, banging pots and pans and the door of the dishwasher, and Shaw returned his attention to the statue glaring at him from the bookcase.

The bird's crest, that cluster of hot pink marble feathers sitting on top of the cockatoo's head, had the tiniest crack along the edge. Even if Shaw had his lab gloves on, he could've felt the defect. That's what he was trained to do. What he prided himself on.

Feeling the defects.

The cockatoo had been a source of consternation when the two were talking marriage and deciding which of her belongings deserved taking up valuable real estate space in her small pair of suitcases. Though adults and perfectly capable of making their own decisions, Shaw and Sharon's trauma likely clouded their judgment. They both knew she needed to make a clean break away from her crazy parents. That meant a drive-through chapel wedding in the city—and packing light.

"But I need it."

"Why, sweetheart? It takes up half your suitcase. You could bring more clothes or books or—"

"This." She'd hugged the cockatoo to her chest and tears streamed down her face. "I can't leave him. I won't."

Though Shaw never understood her attachment to the bird, and she'd never told him, he'd caved, and she'd guarded the statue like it was a child ever since. No matter which room the cockatoo lived in, it was given a place of prominence. In the bedroom it sat on the dresser. In the kitchen, on top of the refrigerator. In the living room, the bird watched the couple as they watched TV or sat on the floor and played Scrabble.

Once in a while, he'd still tease her about the sentiment of it, and every time she'd smile, a little sweet, and a little sour, and one eyebrow would go up all adorable-like and she'd say "Cigar box."

Then he'd nod and drop it. And they'd sweetly go about their business.

As important as the bird was to her, Shaw's cigar box was invaluable to him. It'd been his grandfather's, and even though he'd never been close to the old man, Shaw had a good reason to keep the box—though he'd never shared it with Sharon.

But Shaw hadn't paraded the box from room to room and caused such a drama about it. And it was much smaller than the marble cockatoo. Sharon didn't have to trip around the cigar box. And the cigar box never stared and glared and pointed its sharp beak like the tropical fowl did.

Shaw had kidded her many times that she should name the bird if it was that important. "How about Kevin or Fred or George?"

"No, silly. It's fine without a name." It was her bird, so he let it go. Secretly, though, he named the cockatoo Howard, after her father. Shaw wasn't sure why he hated Cockatoo the Nameless so much, but he was entirely sure why he'd hated Howard the Human.

Shaw leaned close to the shelf and under his breath said to the bird, "You sneaky creep, Howard. You did it, didn't you? And Sharon helped? Huh? Is that why you're living with us?"

"Are you talking to that bird?" Sharon stood in the door between the living room and kitchen holding a bowl of salad greens and looking a mite confused.

Shaw straightened. Smiled. "It's been a really long day, honey. I need to get cleaned up, then I'll join you for dinner." He gave her a peck on one cheek, wiped the flour from her other and went to change clothes. He pulled the bedroom door softly shut behind him. And turned the lock ever so quietly.

He only ever locked the door when he'd had a bad day at work.

And needed to check his cigar box.

First thing this morning, Shaw's boss had rolled in a tote of evidence for Shaw to process. He was to make a 3D rendering and computer images of injuries and compare them to the skull X-rays from some twenty-year-old cold case. That was the backlog on cold cases. Twenty years.

He took off his collared shirt, tossed it into the hamper in the corner and sat on the bed. He opened his nightstand drawer and moved aside copies of sci-fi magazines and receipts from carry-out and oil changes he should've inputted long ago. His cigar box was still there. He pulled it out, opened the lid, and held his breath. Everything was as it had been the last time he'd checked it.

He exhaled, not knowing how long he'd kept the air in his lungs. The skulls from the lab this morning were his parents'. His boss had no idea. Shaw had no idea, either. Not at first. He never looked at the victim's names. He scanned the barcode and then started up the 3D printerand got to work. But the shape and angles of their injuries matched. Matched Howard the Cockatoo's broken crest.

Sharon had freed Shaw.

Inside were his parents' wedding rings, given to him after forensics didn't need them any longer. He placed them on the nightstand.

Grandpa's old pipe came out next. Then a few Polaroids of some long-ago pets and a shot of himself as a toddler on a rickety aluminum swing set.

When the box was empty, he gently pushed the bottom right corner and the wood shifted ever so slightly, revealing a false base.

He lifted the panel up.

They were still there. In a baggie. Nice, flat, white tablets. Tasteless in the right drink. Time-delayed under the right circumstances. He had a few left. Howard the Human never knew what hit him.

Shaw had freed Sharon. It was justified.

He prided himself on the way he treated Sharon.

And Howard the Cockatoo connected Sharon to his parents' death. The broken crest, if he were to make a 3D rendering, he knew, would fit the angles of the fractures in his parents' skulls.

Sharon had freed Shaw. And it was just as justified.

And somehow, the most connected couple in the world had kept these awful secrets from each other—in plain sight—for fifteen years.

Shaw finished getting ready for dinner. He joined his fine wife at the dinner table. He kissed her forehead. Her cheeks. She smiled. He smiled.

"Everything as it should be with the cigar box?" she asked. He startled a bit, his fork loaded with Caesar-drenched greens paused halfway to his mouth. She knew. He took a bite and nodded.

They ate in silence for a while.

"Took you long enough to figure it out. About the bird." Sharon sliced into the pie and slid it onto Shaw's plate.

"I was giving your ratio of lemon-to-meringue the benefit of the doubt." He lied. He'd had no idea until today. She knew he was lying and didn't care. She gave herself a slice.

"You're too sweet."

Then Lemon Meringue and Peaches 'N Cream enjoyed their strawberry pie after a long day of hard work while Howard the Cockatoo waited patiently in the living room for the Scrabble game to start.

THE RELOADER

Emily knew exactly how to care for Hugh, a reclusive man burdened with phobias and insecurities. But when his beloved Emily dies, Hugh must manage their business and his unhinged view of the world all while planning his wife's final arrangements.

The workshop bench called to Hugh. From behind the glass display case with its mini LED track lights tucked inside the corners highlighting various wares and samples. From behind the textured plaster wall painted periwinkle and dappled with prices and offerings. From behind the clock on that blue wall—now with a dark streaky stain—ticking off the time when client-facing hours ceased and the behind-the-scenes work began.

The workbench behind the wall was always his steady friend, away from customers' views, with its cedar beam legs and worn oak top, nicked and rugged. When muffled voices from the shopfront snaked their way past the plaster and beams, he'd lean into the bench a little harder, allowing the wood to press into his stomach, steadying him, and try to isolate only the cadence of Emily's words. The top was worn smooth where the oil from Hugh's tools and hands soaked in along with the scooting and pulling of items across the surface. The constant layer of dust and grit and metal shavings negated the need to sandpaper the workbench top.

Hugh liked his spot with his bench and equipment and ashy existence behind the shop wall. Emily had been the face of their business. The brains. The voice in front of the periwinkle.

The everything.

His everything.

From his bench, with the workroom door open, he could see the front door of the shop. Now he was in the shop. Facing the front. The periwinkle all around him. The dark, round stain by the front door. He'd not figured what he'd tell anyone about it, should they ask. He'd hoped they'd simply not ask.

He'd also hoped, should he have a customer today, that they'd not ask of Emily, either. But he knew they would. She was loved. And she'd be missed.

Hugh hadn't had a single customer today, but he couldn't bring himself to simply leave the shop's front unattended and just go to the bench. Emily blamed that preciseness, that over-the-top rule following, on his obsessive-compulsive disorder. Agoraphobia, specifically.

Disorders. Phobias.

He preferred not to think of his carefulness as a condition.

Just a simple preference to have things a certain way and avoid all interactions with unpredictable people—Emily's spontaneity and creativity gave him a lifetime's worth of unpredictability, he needed no more than that. He'd often wondered why Emily had chosen him.

Was he a problem to solve? Did she truly love him? He truly loved her. Even offered to set her free more than once when the crippling fear settled in and he couldn't so much as walk out the front door of his own home.

She deserved better. To be free.

But she'd stayed. And loved him and cared for him as his wife and business partner.

And, obsessive compulsive disorder or dutiful business owner, he forbade himself from leaving the stool behind the glass case before closing time. He'd crane his neck every five minutes toward the clock in hopes that fifteen or twenty minutes had vanished. He'd wipe the counter down with his microfiber dust rag, removing the dusty remains which inevitably floated into the storefront from his workbench area. Then he'd reposition himself on the stool and start the cycle over again. Until quitting time.

Quitting time when he could work on one simple reload order and one burning.

Nice money.

Filling and burning.

Emily's idea, both of those. When her parents had died in the car crash, the family, including Hugh and the other in-laws, hadn't enough funds even when pooled together to bury the couple. Cremation was also outrageously expensive for what it was, but that's the route the adult children took, each taking turns making unaffordable payments until the funeral bill was paid off.

Then there was the issue of the overly sentimental family

figuring on a common resting place to put the ashes so they could all visit.

So Emily got creative. And her sisters joined in.

Her parents had been hunters. Avid ones, amassing an impressive collection of guns, shells—full and spent—and reloading equipment. Emily carefully funneled her parents' ashen remains into the hollows of shotgun shells. Mixed in gunpowder. Sealed the cartridges.

And, boom!

Each woman fired off as many shots that day as it took to broadly scatter mother and father over the beloved hunting grounds. Emily and her sisters visit that spot each season to pay their respects and share happy memories with picnics, target practice, or simple hikes.

Each season. Four times a year. Without fail.

Without Hugh. Hugh had mustered all he could to manage attendance at the initial "scattering" of the remains. He didn't think he could go to that spot in the woods again and feel the echo of the shotgun blasts down to his toes. To see the nesting birds rise high up in the air from startling footsteps and chattering women.

No, he'd preferred the solitude and to allow Emily the elbow room to jaw it up with her siblings. That'd been a mistake.

Hugh should've gone. Each and every time. Four times a year. For the last six years.

Six times four. Twenty-four.

When had it started?

Another crane of the neck, and the clock graciously dismissed him from his perch. He stood and stretched out the kinks. From his neck. From his legs. Hands. Fingers. He had real work to do now. He rubbed his stomach. Hunger hadn't visited him in quite some time. Emily had always scolded him about his intake. Reminding him when he should eat during those times he became engrossed in the work. Bringing him cold cut sandwiches in the summer or steaming mugs of tomato soup in the winter.

He'd miss that soup. Her soup.

He'd miss her.

He should be grateful for the time he'd had with her. But it had never been enough, as Emily's time had been split, not evenly by any stretch, between the shop and Hugh. The shop won out most of the time. But Hugh usually didn't mind, as he was always close by. Behind the periwinkle wall taking in her muffled condolences to the customers.

Her soft humming as she straightened and cleaned the shopfront.

Her scent of lilacs and vanilla and tomato soup wafting through the open workroom door when the shop was empty.

About the only time Emily left Hugh to himself was on her runs into town to gather supplies or groceries. And those were quick and to the point.

The longest stretches were those trips to the hunting grounds with her sisters.

Hugh stood behind his workbench, the padded mat under his feet remembering exactly where he liked to stand and eased the pressure from his knees. His tools were arranged in precise order, from largest to smallest. A neat curl of periwinkle ribbon, satin and smooth, waited for him at the end of the bench. Waited for Hugh to incorporate it into the final work. He ran the dust rag over the bench and tools, giving all a light brushing, sending the remains of unknown number of folks to the floor in dusty wisps.

He shook his head. How many times had a customer asked if they received "all" of their loved one back. No one ever receives them all back.

Ever.

So Emily lied. And the customer would nod a teary acceptance. And Hugh would say nothing, just bow his head in humble respect during those times when he was within eyeshot of a customer. That customer's loved one was—or would be soon after the pit was fired up—all over the shop's floor. All over the ceiling. The glass case.

Floating in the air.

Stuck to the periwinkle plaster.

And all over Emily and Hugh as they journeyed home each night.

Hugh tried not to think about that part. That someone—in some form or another—was always with him. Maybe that's why eating was such a deal. He knew, even if he didn't dwell on it, that he'd likely consumed bits and pieces of every cremation he'd performed with every meal.

As much as he loved his solitude, he was never, ever alone.

Hugh picked up his funnel and began setting up the reloading station. He had a couple of orders. He'd start with the simplest first. And one that mirrored the first time he'd helped Emily with her crazy business idea.

As word spread regarding Emily's ceremony for her parents, Emily was recruited to do likewise for others' deceased loved ones. Reloading shotgun shells from their kitchen table in their cozy one-bedroom nestled at the side of the lane. Hugh had helped. Happy to be under the same roof as his true love. Happy not to have to leave for a job outside the home. Emily was all he needed.

When the complaining grew over funeral options and expenses in their cash-strapped—and rapidly aging—community, Emily had another idea.

"Hugh. Let's charge. Not a lot. Just cover costs and our simple living expenses. We don't need much, you and I." She'd tousled his hair and sat on his lap. The only human in the world he'd let into his space. "We could offer what the funeral services don't. Creative disposals—past the necklaces and urns. And cremation."

"That's a lot. Why not just keep it simple—"

"Hugh. Diversify or die." She'd kissed him.

And he conceded to Emily's runaway creativity. But, it turned out one must have licenses and certifications and some manner of education to run a crematorium. And a proper setup was cost prohibitive.

They'd sat on the idea. Tossing pros and cons around like hot potatoes around the dinner table. Hugh'd eventually lost interest in the body-burning business. Emily had not. Her passion for the idea burned fresh with each season.

With each trip to the forest with her sisters to pay homage to her gone-too-soon parents. After those long afternoons away from Hugh, she'd come back full of life and vim and hopes and dreams...

And she'd pressed. Carefully. Because she'd known that's how Hugh would respond best. Careful. Calculated. Precise plans.

And, carefully, they began building a rudimentary pit. One that could reach eighteen hundred degrees Fahrenheit and not alert the far-reaching neighbors. One with a specialized grate and pulley system that could be lifted so the cremains could be gathered. Hugh had pointed out this system is flawed. Their cremains wouldn't be pure.

Dear old Aunt Sally goes into the heat, but only a thimbleful of aunt Sally comes out, along with a teaspoon of Fred the butcher and half gallon of the Posey's old cow. That cow that had served the Poseys so well over the last decade and they just couldn't bear the thought of not having something to remember her by—as if the extra rims around their belts from the fresh milk and butter weren't remembrance enough.

Emily had chided him. It was the thought that counted. And if they wanted all their loved one—or beloved pet—they'd have to go through the proper funeral home or veterinary services.

Hugh's fingers flew over the shells and funnels and packs of gunpowder. Setting each one into the press. Sealing the ashes and powder together. For someone's final earthly send-off.

Almost done with the customer's order. He could pay his meager bills for another month with the payment. Five simple shotgun shells. One month of food and electric. Their property had been paid off free and clear. Everything in the couple's name. Emily's doing.

Emily was everywhere.

He tidied up the special order, placed the shells in a simple white box, and tied it shut with a red ribbon. The address on the order indicated that soon he'd hear these five shots echo across the valley. Over his house. Through the trees and down the lane to the secluded shop. Through his bones. Each shot reminded Hugh of the day he'd watched Emily and her sisters fire off their parents.

Between the hunters firing at prey and the reloaded cremation shells ringing through the afternoons, gunfire was a common, unreported occurrence.

The shot from the small crematory business certainly went unreported, or Hugh wouldn't have been able to come to work today.

Hugh readied his apron for the trip to the pit. Death was a nasty thing. Necessitating dust rags, aprons and periwinkle touch-up paint.

From his place on the padded mat, he could see the dark, round stain on the periwinkle plaster to the right of the doorframe. Periwinkle—Emily's favorite color. Nearly the color of her eyes. She'd told Hugh blue made people feel at ease—a comfort color. He enjoyed the walls and had even let her paint the workshop the same hue. He drew comfort from the color, Emily had been correct.

Or maybe because the walls brought out the rich blue of her eyes.

Hugh had allowed his arthritic fingers to linger over that dark, round stain this morning when he opened the shop. It was dry now. He'd not figured out what to do about it yet. He didn't know where Emily kept the periwinkle touch-up paint.

He'd fired up the pit first thing before opening the shop. It needed preheating, so to speak. Hugh had expertly prepped and wrapped the body in a muslin tarp and tied it up with twine yesterday. The mummy form rested on the utility cart all lined with bricks of ice, just now starting to drip. He used industrial tongs to replace the ice blocks back into the freezer. No need to be wasteful.

Hugh rolled the rig out across the yard—a yard so rutted up with mole hills that he'd have to take care not to lose the package on the way to the smoldering pit.

Emily never worried about the smoke from the cremations. Hugh had fretted over it, at first, until Emily solved the problem. They offered free services to the neighboring farmers—the ones most likely to see a billowing cloud rising high into the sky at the edges of their properties. The ones most likely to call the law. And then the couple offered services to the law.

The conservation officer servicing their county had aging parents. And a conservation officer's salary.

The local sheriff had a ninety-three-year-old grandmother. And aging parents. And a small-town elected official's salary.

Emily never felt guilty about billing for the services. The work was worth it. Hugh, now at the deep pit, rolled the body in. The mummy toppled face down into the glowing hole. A dark, round stain had started on the back. Not quite as big as the one on the periwinkle entry wall. He watched for a moment as the muslin caught fire, erasing the stain in hungry flames. He closed the iron lid down tight and walked a few feet further into the yard and opened the oxygen intake. One can't have fire without air.

He turned back to face the porch. The smoke wafted from the ground, stinging his eyes and enveloping him in the familiar gray embrace of a body reclaimed by the elements.

And he swore he saw a wisp of periwinkle braiding with the darker grays from the muslin wrap. He knew that was imagination—a bit of Emily rubbing off on him. A bit too sleep deprived. Blood sugar no doubt dipping.

He walked back inside to his bench and hung up the apron, wet from the melting ice and smokey from the pit. He rested his eyes on the dark, round stain and tried not to relive yesterday's ordeal.

When the young man had brought Emily's phone back.

From the woods.

Where she'd gone to pay her seasonal respects to her parents. With her sisters.

And with this man. Ten years Hugh's junior. Open. Smiling. Bright.

Not riddled with phobias and conditions.

This strange man was free.

And Hugh had decided later that night, after closing time, that Emily needed to be free, too.

He focused down to the workbench. To the empty hourglass. The size of a dollar bill in height and width, the glass supported on either side by slender spindles of oak. The last one in stock.

Emily's favorite piece. She'd filled several of these over the years. "To have them for all time" was her sales pitch. Hugh thought that great. "For all time."

The family chose their loved one's favorite color, and Emily would mingle the colorful grains with the ashen remnants.

Tying a matching ribbon to the middle.

He had a few hours—two, probably, from the size of the body—to wait until he could gather the remains and give them a proper final resting place in the hourglass. He opened the stopper on the bottom of the piece and poured in periwinkle blue sand.

A peaceful color. Emily's favorite. It would blend well with the ashy gray of her remains. Mimicking the flecks of gray in her eyes. He returned the stopper and tipped the hourglass on its opposite site. He stared as the sand grains jostled for position at the narrow neck between the glass bulbs.

Gray and blue. Blue and gray.

It was missing something. Hugh had always thought the hourglass mementos missed something. Two-tone and lacking depth. He glanced up to the stain on the wall. Darker blue than the surrounding plaster after the scrubbing down.

He chose a long metal file from the line of tools on his bench. He wiped each side of the file on his pant leg, removing a thin, ever-collecting layer of dust. He removed the stopper from the hourglass once again and took both items to the wall.

To the stain.

Hugh scraped the plaster, the darker blue stain, in fine dusty chunks into the hourglass with the periwinkle blue sand.

He stopped filing when he reached bare wall and enough particles had entered the tiny hole in the hourglass to appease him. The rest he left in a mess on the floor, on his arms, on his pant legs.

With the dust rag, he cleaned up the outside of the hourglass. He replaced the stopper again and twisted and turned the piece to watch a more interesting show. More varied. More creative.

Like his Emily.

As Hugh picked up the satin ribbon, he had second thoughts. Maybe he should reload her. Pack some shells and send her off to be with her parents. He could do that. Manage one more trip to the woods to give Emily a final, free resting place.

But Hugh never liked sharing. He only ever shared with Emily. He let the ribbon dangle in his fingertips.

And if Hugh put Emily there, in that spot that she so eagerly shared with this other man each season, then Hugh would be sharing Emily in the rawest sense.

No.

Hugh tied the periwinkle ribbon to the slender part of the hourglass and removed the stopper. He placed the tip of the smallest funnel he had into the hole.

No.

He and the hourglass would wait for the pit to do its job.

And Hugh would keep Emily to himself for all time.

LAKE GEORGE

When the latest in a series of abductions takes Carrie Wheeler—a young girl with freckles and red hair, just like the others—there is little hope of finding the perpetrator at all, let alone in time to save the girl's life. For the world-weary detective assigned to the case, the statistics are unassailable: the girl is as good as gone. Still, you do the work and if you're lucky, at the end of the day, you get a little time to spend with your loved ones.

The scene may change, but the undercurrent stays the same. The families look to me for guidance, while at the same time loathing the fact that I won't let them have a moment to grieve and gather their thoughts. There are two reasons for that.

Giving them time allows the gathering of thoughts and alibis, if one of them is to blame.

Giving them time ticks away seconds that their daughter may not have.

There's never enough time.

The curly, red-headed child, Carrie, smiled back at me from the family photo, removed from its silver frame on the mantelpiece just moments ago. Freckled cheeks, green eyes full of hope and wonder.

Just like the first two.

The hamster wheel spins again and it seems there is no way to stop it.

Mom sobs. Dad blames mom for allowing the outing in the first place. Aunt was the last to see the child on the carousel, bobbing up and down on the pink horse with the purple mane. One turn of the ride, she was there, giggling.

The next she wasn't.

We locked down the traveling carnival to question the onlookers and carnies. Most of my guys were still at the scene. We brought in the dogs to search the wooded area next to the park.

We won't find anything. Not today.

I traveled back to the family's home with the parents for questioning.

They showed me the little girl's room, a perfect balance of ruffles, pinks and yellows, with stuffed animals and dress-up clothes. On her nightstand, a porcelain box with glittered purple wings held her first tooth she lost just this morning. The Tooth Fairy would visit tonight.

Or would have.

"Detective Sanders, please, please. I know what happened to those other children—"

"Actually, ma'am, we don't know what happened to the others. Don't let your mind go there. You contacted us real quick, so that's something. I need you to concentrate on the facts, please."

I lied. I did know. I know the statistics. The odds. The chances. Whatever you want to call it. I just know.

The chances of finding Carrie, or Tessa or Emma, were slim. In the course of a year, three gingers disappeared from three states, all from traveling carnivals. All from the carousel.

At this stage, with this many missing, we don't tell the families we're not looking for their child. In reality, we're gathering patterns and dots on a map and data to try to capture the abductor.

"Mr. Wheeler, could you tell me what your daughter's favorite foods are, favorite toys, anything like that?" And then I wait. It will dawn on them how useless that question seems.

He fumbled and rubbed his hands through his graying red hair. "I, um..."

"It's okay. Take your time."

"I..., well, she likes hot dogs, and—" And then it happened. "What does that matter? Shouldn't you be out there looking? *I* should be out there looking." He tried to brush past me, but I caught him by the shoulders and led him to the sofa.

"If she has a peculiar interest, the abductor may make certain purchases. It could help us locate her. Please." I motioned for a junior detective. "Please, you and your wife tell Detective Grant everything you can think of about Carrie. Don't hold anything back." The grief-worn couple nodded and Grant sat on the coffee table in front of them, taking down everything they said. I'd get her notes later.

I went to the front porch where the aunt was smoking a cigarette and nursing a Miller Light.

"Can you drink that and remain clear enough to answer my questions?"

She gave me an eat-crap-and-die look. I let her keep it.

I started the same routine questions with her as I had with the parents. And the carousel operator. And the park director. Nothing new would turn up from this, but it was procedure. I put another junior on her and took a ride to the park.

Back in the nineties, we caught an abduction case similar to this. Five boys taken at bus stops in larger cities. With each case, the parents grew more frantic because they knew the previous boys hadn't been located.

Until we did locate all of them after the perp bought the last boy his favorite candy, Necco Wafers. A gas station clerk saw the news and called it in, and the perp was arrested twenty minutes later. The fifth boy was returned unscathed.

The other four were found in the perp's wood shed. Very much scathed.

The park looked as it should. A line of onlookers three deep, trying to catch a glimpse of something to talk about over dinner. Trying to be a part of things. Cell phones up, recording and photographing. Two deputies held them back with yellow painted sawhorses.

Over the rest of the grounds my team had scattered in all directions, searching with dogs and dusting the carousel. Most of them knew it was futile, but they did the work nonetheless.

I walked along the edge of the wooded ravine. Others of my team had dogs in full-out sprints, all of them whining and barking, but none of them signaling "found her."

Someone handed me a zipped baggie with Carrie's green and purple pajamas that she'd worn last night. The mother had fished them out of the laundry for the search team. We also took her toothbrush and hairbrush. In case we needed to compare remains later.

I sat down on the bench facing the carousel. A pair of officers was subduing the angry carnival manager and his employee. They wanted to leave. But clearing names takes time.

I focused on the notes I'd written so far. I'd gather everyone's notes later and go over them in my hotel room off Route 45.

A junior sat next to me. "Think we'll get him this time?"

I rested my elbows on my knees and put my head in my hands. "No."

"I hope you're not this optimistic with the family."

"We had five extra hours with Tessa. Seven with Emma. We're hours behind. He's slick. We won't find him because he hasn't made a mistake," I snapped back, and the junior left me alone.

The investigation needed a Necco Wafer moment.

———

The hotel's ancient AC unit rattled against the wall and the flow split open the drapes so that I got an occasional glimpse at the rain pouring down the window. Another setback. Any evidence that was missed today would be gone tomorrow.

My phone had gone off a dozen times in the last hour. A tidbit here, a morsel there. Nothing that mattered in the long run.

The aunt has a history of alcoholism. The dad lost his job a few weeks ago. Mom had needed a break from the energetic six-year-old and allowed her sister, sober this morning, to accompany Carrie to the carnival. And the blame game starts. And the guilt.

I spread out the notes on the brown bedspread. Most of her interests and likes were that of any little girl her age. Everything except the candy. I picked up the phone and dialed the press liaison.

"Yeah, Melissa. Give this to the news. Carrie Wheeler's favorite candy bar is a Zero." I flung the phone on the bed and lay across sideways on my back. The popcorn ceiling needed a paint job. I was thankful I wouldn't be here much longer.

Tomorrow I'd drive across two state lines back to my home to work remotely. My wife missed me. She said so in her texts. But things were going just fine at the lake with the kids.

It was the same lake where we lost our little girl years ago, but no investigation was started. We watched it happen right before our eyes. She was there, bobbing up and down in the water one minute, and the next she wasn't.

I do know what the families feel.

I don't know what they feel not knowing. I couldn't stand the not knowing.

I rolled off the bed and headed for the shower.

One more day on the hamster wheel. Then I get to see my family.

After condolences, directions and orders were handed out, I drove away from the Wheelers' home—for the last time unless any new evidence showed up. My job starts in earnest when I get back to home base.

Data is my playground. Patterns and habits and routes and maps. I prefer to let someone else handle the people.

I texted Heather to see if she or the kids needed anything. She texted back a list of a few odds and ends. I stopped at a convenience store about ten miles from the lake. It was well stocked and even had a small souvenir section for the one-time campers with post cards and hats. I picked up the foodstuffs and a tiny box caught my eye. It was made of wood and *Lake George* was burned into the hinged lid. I opened it. It was lined with red cloth. On the bottom it said *Made in China*. But it would do.

I checked out and noticed the Necco Wafers.

And a Zero bar.

I tossed three bags of M&Ms on the counter for the kids and a Dove bar for Heather.

At the house, I was greeted by two of my kids and my wife. The third child sat sucking her thumb in the corner of the couch.

"I have candy!" I handed out two M&Ms and the Dove. Squeals of laughter and quick hugs and the older two were off to see who had the most red candies.

"She hasn't said anything."

"She'll be fine." I brushed back Heather's long red hair behind her ear and kissed her freckled cheek. "It just takes time." I went to the couch.

I offered the tiny girl the bag of candy and she shook her head. I left it on the couch.

I offered her the Lake George box. She didn't take it, but I had her attention. I rattled the box. Her eyes widened somewhat.

She took her spit-soaked hand and held the box. With the other, she slowly opened the lid. She looked at me with her piercing green eyes and the corners of her mouth drew up ever so slightly.

"Do you think the Tooth Fairy can find you now?"

About the Author

Beth enjoys chucking words into sentences then standing back to see what magic—or mayhem—falls out, crafting tales in mystery, sci-fi, fantasy, and general "slice of life" fiction. She couldn't accomplish this without the help of her tutu-clad Little Miss Muse and Trudi the Concrete Office Goose, who's partial to superhero capes.

Her stories have appeared in multiple publications, including Pulphouse Fiction Magazine and Ellery Queen Mystery Magazine, and in multiple fiction anthologies. She's received several Honorable Mentions from Writers of the Future. Her lighthearted blog peeks into the writing life as she pokes fun at herself and her circus of a life.

Follow the antics of Little Miss Muse and Trudi, read Beth's blog (she might have burned down her kitchen last week), and discover the stories at bapaul.com.

Also by B. A. Paul

Short Story Collections

Spunk and Spice, Volumes 1 and 2: A Collection of six short stories celebrating timeless wit and wisdom.

Out There, Volumes 1 and 2: A Collection of six short sci-fi and speculative tales.

Mystery Minutes, Volumes 1 and 2: Six short mystery stories

All the Feels, Volumes 1, 2, and 3: Collections of inspiring short stories

Just a Tick of Whimsy, Volumes 1 and 2: Collections of fantasy shorts.

Hijacked Holidays: Definitely not your warm-and-fuzzy winter tales.

Dark Minds: Toe-curling twisted mysteries.

Blog Compilations: Slices of the writing life with lots of laughs and bumps in the road.

Life Along the Way

Life All Over Again

Novels

Triage

Young Adult (or Young at Heart) Books

Switch: Book 1 in the Oliver Andrews Trilogy

Stay In Touch!

BAPAUL.COM

Take a glimpse into B.A. Paul's writing journey, including the ups and downs of managing family, "real jobs," ducks in wobbling rows, and chasing down her Little Miss Muse. New blog posts go up Mondays, with the first Monday of the Month reserved for a free fiction short story available on the blog for a limited time.

Newsletter Signup Coming in 2021!

Get the latest release information, author updates, and exclusive content. Details to come! Follow the blog or Facebook for more announcements regarding the newsletter.

www.ingramcontent.com/pod-product-compliance
Lightning Source LLC
Chambersburg PA
CBHW070355310726
48977CB00002B/453